of the
lost words

ASHWINI PRATHAM

notionpress
.com

INDIA · SINGAPORE · MALAYSIA

"Some love stories endure beyond the lives that lived them, woven into the fabric of generations that follow. They pass down as whispers, as longings we don't understand, as echoes in our hearts–binding us to those who came before and inspiring us to find a love that leaves its own mark on time."

Whispers in the Dust

T he monsoon clouds loomed heavily over Mumbai, casting a grey hue over the bustling city streets. Aanya Sharma sat by the window of her modest apartment, the first droplets of rain splattering against the glass. There was a comfort in watching the city blur in the downpour, rickshaws splashing through puddles, people running for shelter, and the occasional laughter of children who found joy in the rain. It was a scene that brought her a strange sense of solace, a reminder of simpler times when watching the rain was a cherished pastime rather than a brief distraction from the chaos within.

The aroma of wet earth mixed with the rich scent of masala chai steaming in her cup. Aanya took a sip, letting the warmth spread through her, but today, it felt hollow. It had been a week since her grandmother, Savitri Sharma, had passed away peacefully in her sleep. The funeral rites were over, relatives had returned to their homes, and now, the void Savitri left behind was settling into Aanya's heart like an unwelcome visitor.

Savitri had been more than a grandmother. She was a confidante, a storyteller, and a custodian of traditions. She was someone Aanya could always rely on, and in her presence, life had felt a little less chaotic. Dadi's stories were an anchor–a thread that connected Aanya to her roots. Without her, the apartment seemed emptier, and Mumbai's noise couldn't fill that silence. Dadi's laughter, her wise eyes, the way she would hold Aanya's hand when she felt lost–these were the things Aanya missed most.

The last few days had been a blur–calls from distant relatives offering condolences, the endless rituals, and her mother's weary, tearful face. Aanya had gone through it all like she was in a daze, her emotions tangled and confused. She knew grief was supposed to feel heavy, like an unbearable weight on her chest, but for Aanya, it felt more like a hollow emptiness. Something crucial had been taken from her, leaving behind a void that she wasn't sure how to fill.

Her phone buzzed on the coffee table, breaking her thoughts. It was a message from her mother, Meera.

"Don't forget to go through Dadi's things at the old house. We need to decide what to keep and what to donate."

Aanya stared at the message, her heart sinking. The thought of going through her grandmother's belongings felt like a daunting task, as though she would be rummaging through her memories, opening wounds that had barely begun to heal. She sighed, fingers hovering over the keypad. A part of her didn't want to face it, the idea of sorting through Dadi's things made her feel like she was erasing her, one item at a time. But it had to be done, and perhaps, just perhaps, it might be a way to reconnect with the memories they had shared.

"I'll go tomorrow morning."

She sent the message and set her phone aside, watching the raindrops roll down the window. Maybe, just maybe, going through her grandmother's things would be a way to feel close to her again—a way to understand a part of her life that Aanya had never known.

The rain continued to pour, the city outside shrouded in mist. Aanya got up from her chair and walked over to the bookshelf. She ran her fingers over the spines of her favourite novels, books that had been gifted to her by Dadi over the years, each one carefully chosen, each one inscribed with a message that reflected Dadi's love for her. She pulled out a book of Hindi poetry and opened the front cover.

"To my dear Aanya, may you always find beauty in the words of others, as you do in the world around you."

Aanya smiled, tears welling in her eyes. Dadi had always known just what to say to make her feel understood. She closed the book gently and placed it back on the shelf. Tomorrow, she would go to the old house. Maybe she would find something there that would bring her closer to Dadi again.

The next morning, Aanya stood in front of the ancestral home in Bandra, an old relic amidst the ever-growing modernity of Mumbai. The two-storey house had faded turquoise walls, its wooden shutters worn from years of enduring rain and sun, and a wrought-iron gate that creaked in protest as she pushed it open. The house stood like a silent sentinel, a witness to the lives that had passed through it, refusing to be swallowed by the world of new apartment complexes and trendy cafes around it.

Aanya paused at the threshold, taking in the familiar scent of sandalwood and something earthy. The house smelled of memories of old books, nostalgia captured in worn-out furniture and lace curtains. She had spent much of her childhood here, running up and down the stairs, hiding behind the heavy drapes, and listening to Dadi's stories of gods and goddesses, heroes and villains. It was a place where her imagination had been allowed to run free.

She pushed the door open, stepping inside. The dust had settled over everything, and as sunlight filtered through the windows, it illuminated particles floating in the air, making them dance. The sitting area was just as she remembered: the worn-out sofa with its embroidered cushions, the rocking chair where Dadi used to sit, knitting sweaters for the winter that Mumbai never saw. Aanya would sit at her feet, listening to stories of far-off lands and brave princesses.

She could almost hear her grandmother's voice, the gentle cadence of her words, the way she would pause for effect, her eyes twinkling with mischief. Aanya moved through the rooms, her fingers brushing over the walls, trailing over the framed photographs that lined the hallway. There was a photograph of her grandfather, Rajesh Sharma, standing beside a young Savitri, their smiles radiant. She lingered on it, tracing the outline of her grandmother's face. Dadi had been beautiful in her youth—her hair thick and dark, her eyes bright with hope.

Aanya found herself wondering about the life she had lived, the dreams she had once had before she became the grandmother Aanya knew.

The kitchen was empty, but the ghost of its past seemed to linger, the smell of freshly made besan laddoos and the clinking of bangles as Dadi stirred a pot on the stove. Aanya remembered standing by her side, watching in awe as her grandmother cooked, her hands moving with practised ease, adding just the right amount of spices. Dadi had always made cooking look effortless, as though it was a form of art, and Aanya had loved being her little helper, measuring out ingredients, tasting the dishes, and learning the secrets of flavours that made every meal special. She smiled at the memory, the warmth of it filling her for a moment. She wished she could go back to those days, just for a moment, to hear Dadi's voice again, to feel the comfort of her presence.

Aanya made her way upstairs to her grandmother's bedroom, her steps slow as she reached the door. She paused her hand on the doorknob, a mix of emotions swirling inside her. This was where Dadi had spent her last days, where she had lived her life, alone but content, surrounded by her books and memories. She pushed the door open, stepping inside. The room was frozen in time, untouched since the day Dadi had left it. The large four-poster bed stood at the centre, draped with an embroidered quilt. A dressing table cluttered with antique jewellery, bottles of perfume, and a mirror that had seen decades of life. The shelves were filled with books, their spines worn with love—poetry in Hindi and English, stories of gods and kings. Aanya found herself drawn to the books, running her fingers over their spines, feeling the years of love her grandmother had poured into them. Aanya walked over to the closet and opened it. Inside were sarees of every fabric—silk, cotton, chiffon—neatly folded, each one with a story of its own. She ran her fingers over them, her heart heavy. She couldn't bring herself to decide what to keep and what to let go. Not yet. She pulled out a bright red silk saree, the one Dadi had worn at Aanya's cousin's wedding. She could almost see her grandmother, her face glowing with happiness, her laughter echoing through the room.

Her eyes drifted to the wooden trunk at the foot of the bed. It was old, with brass fittings tarnished from age and intricate carvings of peacocks and lotus flowers. Aanya knelt beside it, running her fingers over the designs, feeling the rough edges beneath her fingertips. She had always been fascinated by the trunk, even as a child, imagining it held treasures from another time. She lifted the lid, and it creaked open as if reluctant to reveal its secrets. Inside were stacks of letters tied with red thread, sepia-toned photographs, trinkets, an old silver hairpin, a broken bangle, and a pressed rose that had lost its colour. Aanya carefully picked up a photograph of her grandmother as a young woman, standing beside a man she didn't recognise. They were smiling, their eyes filled with a kind of joy that seemed to belong to another world. "Who are you?" Aanya whispered, tracing the outline of the man's face with her thumb.

Beneath the photographs lay a leather-bound journal, its edges frayed, and it was secured with a delicate brass lock. Aanya's heart skipped a beat. She had never seen her grandmother write in a diary. There was something intimate about it, something that called to her, like a whisper from the past. She hesitated for a moment, staring at the small lock that held the secrets of a life she had never known. She searched the trunk for a key but found none. Determined, she tried to pry it open gently, but the lock held firm. Frustrated but intrigued, she placed the diary on the bed and continued rummaging through the trunk.

She wasn't ready to give up on uncovering this hidden side of her grandmother just yet.

At the very bottom, wrapped in a silk cloth, was a small wooden box. Her fingers trembled as she opened it. Inside lay a brass key, intricately designed with patterns that matched those on the trunk. Aanya's breath caught in her throat.

Could this be it?

"Could this be the key?" she wondered aloud, her voice barely a whisper.

Her heart pounded in anticipation as she picked up the key. She inserted it into the lock of the diary, her fingers trembling. With a soft click, the lock opened. Aanya hesitated, her heart pounding in her chest. Part of her felt like she was intruding on her grandmother's private thoughts, but a stronger part of her felt that Dadi would have wanted her to find this, to understand her in a way no one else had. Taking a deep breath, she opened the first page, her eyes scanning the delicate, handwritten words.

"To my dearest Aanya,

If you're reading this, it means I've embarked on my next journey. There are stories untold, secrets kept, and truths buried that I wish to share with you. This diary holds the whispers of my past, a past that is as much yours as it is mine."

Aanya's eyes welled with tears, her fingers brushing over the words. It was as if her grandmother was speaking to her, guiding her, even now. She could almost hear Dadi's voice in her head, the warmth and love she had always offered so generously. Aanya turned the page, eager to delve into the world her grandmother had preserved within these pages.

"5ᵗʰ June 1952

Nandipur is unlike any place I've known. The fields stretch endlessly, the Ganges flow with a serenity that calms the soul, and the banyan tree stands tall, guarding the secrets of the village. Today, I met someone who changed everything…"

Nandipur. The name struck a chord in Aanya's memory, a distant familiarity. She recalled the stories her grandmother used to tell her as a child, stories of a village by the river, of fields that stretched as far as the eye could see. She had always thought they were just tales, not real places. It was a place from a different time, a place that existed only in the words of her grandmother, and now here it was, brought to life in her diary. She continued reading, and each entry painted vivid pictures of life in Nandipur, the festivals, the people, and the traditions. The diary was filled with descriptions of colourful celebrations, of dances under the moonlight, of the simple joys of life in a village that seemed almost untouched by time. Aanya felt herself being transported to that world, imagining her grandmother as a young girl, filled with hope and wonder.

And then, a name appeared again and again: Dev. *"Dev is different from the others. He listens when I speak, truly listens. His eyes hold a depth that draws me in, and his laughter is like music. I think, perhaps, I am falling in love…"* Aanya felt a pang of emotion and curiosity mixed with something deeper.

Who was Dev? Her grandfather's name was Rajesh, and he had passed away before she was born. She had never heard of anyone named Dev in her grandmother's life. What had happened between them? Why had Dadi never spoken of him? She turned the page, eager to learn more.

"14ᵗʰ August 1952

Under the banyan tree, Dev and I shared our dreams. He spoke of travelling the world, of writing poetry that could move mountains. I told him about my desire to teach and

inspire young minds. We carved our initials into the roots, a
promise to never forget this moment."

Aanya closed the diary momentarily, her heart racing.
This was a side of her grandmother she had never known,
a young woman in love, full of dreams and hope. She
could almost see them under the banyan tree, the sunlight
filtering through the leaves, the promise of a future together
in their eyes.

She spent the next few hours lost in the diary, oblivious
to the world around her. The entries became more intense,
filled with clandestine meetings, whispered conversations,
and plans for a future together. Dev was her grandmother's
world, her escape from the constraints of a society that
sought to keep them apart. Aanya could feel the love that
bound them, the passion and the determination to be
together despite all odds. But then, the tone shifted.

"30th September 1952

Our families have forbidden us from seeing each other. They
say our union is impossible and that society would never
accept it. Dev belongs to a different caste, and traditions
bind us more tightly than any chain."

Aanya's heart ached for her grandmother. She knew
all too well the rigid societal structures that persisted in
parts of India. It was painful to think that love could be
snatched away simply because of something as arbitrary as

caste. She wondered how it must have felt for Dadi to be torn away from the person she loved, to have her dreams shattered by the weight of tradition and expectation.

"15ᵗʰ October 1952

We have decided to leave Nandipur. Under the cover of darkness, we will make our way to Kolkata and start anew. It's risky, but love gives us courage."

"17ᵗʰ October 1952

The moon was a faint crescent, barely lighting our path as Dev and I crept through the narrow lanes of Nandipur, our footsteps muffled by the soft earth. My heart raced—not out of fear, but anticipation. Freedom felt so close, just a train ride away. Dev held my hand tightly, his grip steady and reassuring.

'Just a little further,' he whispered, his voice cutting through the stillness of the night.

But fate has its own plans, doesn't it? As we reached the edge of the village, a shadow emerged from the banyan tree, followed by another. My father's voice thundered through the darkness. 'Savitri!'

Dev's hand slipped from mine as my uncles and cousins surrounded us, their voices sharp and accusing. They dragged Dev away, their hands rough against his arms.

I screamed and begged them to stop, but my voice was drowned in their rage.

'You have brought shame upon this family!' my father spat, his eyes burning with fury.

Dev fought to free himself, his eyes locked on mine. 'Run, Savitri! Go!' he shouted.

But how could I? How could I leave him behind? My father grabbed my arm, his grip like iron, and pulled me back toward the village. Tears streamed down my face as I watched them drag Dev away, his voice echoing in the night. I didn't know where they took him. I didn't know if I would ever see him again. All I knew was that our dreams of a life together had been crushed in an instant, and the weight of my family's honour now chained me to a future I had never chosen."

Aanya turned the next page, but it was torn halfway through. The following entries were sparse and disjointed.

" 28th October, 1952

I have spent days locked in my room, my tears soaking the pillow that once brought me comfort. The silence in the house is unbearable. Every time I close my eyes, I see him— his smile, his outstretched hand, the life we had dreamed of together.

Chandrika Tai came to see me today. She sat by my side, her hand warm on mine, her presence steady. She didn't speak for a long time, allowing my sobs to echo in the quiet of the room. When she finally did, her words cut through my despair.

'Savitri, you have always been stronger than you believe,' she said, her voice firm but kind. 'What has happened cannot be undone, but you must think of your future and your safety. Rajesh is a good man. He will take care of you, and in time, you will find your place.'

I shook my head, my voice trembling. 'But what of love, Tai? What of the life I wanted?'

She sighed, her eyes filled with both sorrow and understanding. 'Love is not always a choice we get to make. Sometimes, survival comes first. You must trust me, Savitri. Marry Rajesh. He will protect you, and you will find peace.'

Her words felt like a betrayal, but deep down, I knew she was right. My family would never allow me to be with Dev, and staying in this house, in this village, would only bring me more pain. I agreed, though my heart screamed against it. I agreed because I had no other choice."

As Aanya closed the diary, her thoughts lingered on the name Chandrika Tai. Who was this woman who had been such a pivotal figure in her grandmother's life? The way Savitri wrote about her made it clear that Chandrika

Tai wasn't just an elder offering advice. She had been a guide in moments of despair, someone whose words carried enough weight to steer Dadi towards an entirely different life.

Turning back to the diary, Aanya noticed there were more torn pages scattered throughout. The gaps in the narrative only deepened her curiosity, leaving her with fragments of a story that begged to be pieced together. What secrets lay in the missing words? What moments had been too painful—or too precious—for Savitri to preserve?

" *2nd November 1952*

Dev is gone. Ever since I told him about my marriage to Rajesh, a silence has settled between us, one too heavy to break. He doesn't come to the banyan tree anymore and doesn't look for me in the village as he used to. It's as if he's slowly slipping away, retreating into a place where I can't follow. I knew this moment would come, but I didn't expect the emptiness it would leave behind. I don't know if I'll ever see him again or if he'll ever forgive me for choosing the path I was bound to follow."

" *10th November, 1952*

They say he's dead. I refuse to believe it. Hope is all I have left."

The final entry was a poem filled with longing and sorrow.

"Whispers of the wind carry your name,

In echoes of the night,

I bear the shame.

Beneath the moon, our promises lie,

In shadows deep, I hear your cry."

Tears streamed down Aanya's face as she read the words. She felt a deep connection to her grandmother, a shared pain that transcended time, a story that had been hidden for far too long. It wasn't just a story of love lost; it was the story of her grandmother's strength, her resilience in the face of heartbreak. She gently closed the diary, her mind swirling with questions. Why had her grandmother never mentioned Dev? What happened to him? And why had her family forced her into an arranged marriage with Dada? Aanya knew one thing for certain–she needed to find answers. Perhaps the key lay in Nandipur, the village her grandmother had loved and lost. As the sun began to set, Aanya left the house, the diary clutched tightly in her hands. This was something she had to do, and she knew she couldn't ignore the call of the past. Somewhere in those words, in those memories, was the key to understanding the woman who had raised her. And maybe, just maybe, it was also the key to understanding herself.

That night, Aanya sat by her window, the city lights shimmering in the rain. Her thoughts drifted to the man in the photograph, the way her grandmother's eyes had looked when she was with him–alive and full of hope. It was a story that had never been told, a love that had been lost to time.

She picked up her phone and called her mother.

"Mom, I want to go to Nandipur."

There was a pause on the other end. "Nandipur? Why?"

"I found Dadi's diary. There are things I need to understand – things she never told us."

"Aanya, your grandmother left that place for a reason. It was too painful for her."

"Maybe," Aanya said, her voice firm, "but I need to know. I need to understand her better."

There was a long silence before her mother spoke again. "Be careful, Aanya. And let me know if you need anything."

"I will, Mom. I promise."

Aanya didn't know what she would find in Nandipur, but she knew she had to go. She had to uncover the truth to give her grandmother's story the ending it deserved.

And perhaps, along the way, she would find something she had been missing all her life – an understanding of who she was and where she came from.

Echoes of a Forgotten Pen

T he next morning dawned with a pale, hesitant light filtering through Mumbai's monsoon clouds, casting a muted glow over the city. She sat on her bed, the diary resting on her lap, feeling the weight of the day ahead.

The world outside her window was just beginning to stir, but inside, her thoughts ran in circles around the revelations in the diary. She flipped through the pages once more, letting Dadi's words wash over her. The entries now felt like a personal invitation into a hidden world where Dadi had once lived out a love story woven with as much loss as beauty. This story, so carefully locked away all her life, now reached across time, binding Aanya to a woman she'd never fully known.

The rain had softened into a mist, making the streets below gleam with a soft sheen. She watched as early morning commuters hurried along the wet pavement, umbrellas and raincoats peppering the scene with bursts of colour. There was a quiet resolve within her now, like the calm that settles after a storm. Today, she would begin to bridge the gap between her world and Dadi's, carrying with her the weight of untold dreams.

She felt a pang of uncertainty—almost fear—at the thought of what she might find. But something in her heart urged her forward, a gentle but insistent pull as if the journey wasn't just for Dadi but also for herself. She needed to understand this love that had so profoundly shaped the woman who had, in turn, shaped her.

Packing felt surreal, and each item she placed in her bag brought her closer to her departure. She moved slowly, taking deliberate care with every fold, every clasp. Her notebook lay ready, and a pen slipped into its spine; she wanted to capture each detail of the journey and create her own record of this passage between past and present. She packed her camera, too, feeling a slight thrill at the thought of photographing Nandipur through her own lens, capturing whatever remnants of Dadi's life she could find there.

And then, the diary. She placed it carefully, as though it were something fragile, a guide that would lead her towards the answers she sought. The leather felt warm under her fingertips, and she couldn't help but wonder how often Dadi had held it, pouring her thoughts into the pages with the hope that someone, someday, would understand.

With her bag packed, she paused at the door, casting a last look at her apartment. The familiar hum of the city drifted through her window, and she closed her eyes, inhaling the faint scent of sandalwood that lingered in the room.

She picked up her phone, dialling her mother one last time before she left. Her mother's voice was soft, almost hesitant. "Are you all set, beta?"

"Yes, Mom," Aanya replied, a warmth spreading through her as she heard the concern in her mother's voice. "I'm ready."

There was a pause. "Be safe, Aanya. And remember... you're not alone. Your father and I are here, whatever you find."

Aanya nodded, swallowing back the wave of emotion. "Thank you, Mom. I'll be okay."

She ended the call, her heart brimming with gratitude. It was strange how Dadi's story was bringing her closer to her mother, to a family history she had only ever glimpsed before. She could feel the generations of women before her, each one carrying her own dreams and heartaches, all woven together like the threads of a single, unbreakable fabric.

As she stepped out into the rainy Mumbai morning, the city greeted her with a kind of quiet acceptance, as if it, too, understood the journey she was undertaking.

She flagged down a rickshaw, the driver nodding politely as she climbed in, her bag carefully placed beside her.

The streets rushed by in a blur of wet pavement and flashing colours, a symphony of life that contrasted sharply with the quiet, timeless village she envisioned in her mind. Nandipur felt both close and distant, a place suspended in her imagination, waiting for her to breathe life back into its forgotten stories.

Mumbai Central Station was a sea of people, all moving with purpose, their faces focused, their bodies weaving in and out of the crowd. The blaring announcements, the clamour of hawkers selling chai and snacks, the sound of a hundred conversations blending into a cacophony, Aanya took a deep breath and adjusted her bag, her eyes scanning the platform until she found hers. The train to Varanasi was waiting, its engine humming as passengers boarded. She checked her ticket again, even though she already knew the details by heart, and made her way to the platform.

She found her seat by the window and settled in, placing her bag on the overhead rack. The compartment slowly filled with travellers: families, young couples, older women dressed in brightly coloured sarees, and a few tourists looking lost. The air was filled with a mix of excitement and exhaustion, the sounds of conversations blending with the announcements echoing through the station. Aanya leaned back in her seat, her heart pounding in her chest. She wondered what she would find in Nandipur. Would there be people who remembered her grandmother? Would anyone remember Dev? Would she find the answers that had eluded her since she first read those words in the diary?

The train began to move, a gentle jerk that set the compartment into motion, and Aanya watched as the platform began to slide away, the station fading into the distance. She could feel the pull of the unknown, the thrill of stepping into a story that had only just begun. And with that thrill came fear, fear of what she might discover, of what she might have to confront. But she knew there was no turning back now.

She was pulled from her thoughts when she heard her name being called. She turned, startled, and saw a familiar face moving towards her.

"Rohan?" she said, her eyes widening in surprise.

It was Rohan Mehra, the young man who lived next door. His tousled hair was as unruly as ever, and he was carrying a backpack that looked as though it had seen a fair share of adventures.

"Hey, Aanya," he greeted her, his smile cheeky. "Fancy running into you here."

"What are you doing here?" Aanya asked, her surprise quickly turning into confusion. "Are you travelling too?"

Rohan dropped his bag onto the seat across from hers, a mix of warmth and hesitation in his eyes. "Actually, your mom called me last night," he admitted. "She told me about your trip to Nandipur and was worried. She had a bad feeling about it and asked me to come along just to make sure you were safe."

Aanya's brows knitted together as she processed his words. "She called you? I only told her about this trip yesterday."

Rohan nodded, his expression softening. "I know. She seemed really concerned. I think she just wanted someone familiar to be with you, given how sudden this all is."

Aanya paused, unsure how to feel. She had planned to do this alone, just her and her grandmother's memories. But there was a strange sense of reassurance in having Rohan beside her, especially considering the uncertainties ahead.

She gave him a small smile. "I guess I could use some help. Thanks."

Rohan's face lit up. "Great! Don't worry; I promise I won't get in your way. Just thought it might be good to have someone along who knows their way around."

Aanya turned her gaze back to the window. The platform began to move out of view, and she felt a sense of finality, leaving behind the familiar and stepping into the unknown. She could feel Rohan's eyes on her, and she wondered what he thought of all this, of her sudden decision to follow a story from the past, a story that wasn't even her own but felt like an essential piece of herself.

The train picked up speed, the landscape outside slowly shifting from the crowded streets of Mumbai to the expanse of green fields and distant hills. Aanya watched as the world blurred by, her thoughts drifting to the entries in the diary. Dev. Nandipur. The banyan tree. She had a feeling that if she could just find the tree, maybe she would find a piece of her grandmother she had never known, a piece of her own history that had been hidden away.

"So," Rohan said after a while, breaking the silence. "Are you going to tell me why you're going to Nandipur?"

Aanya looked at him, her eyes searching his face. There was no judgement there, only curiosity. She hesitated for a moment, then reached into her bag and pulled out the photograph of her grandmother and Dev. She handed it to Rohan.

He studied it for a moment, then looked up at her. "Who's the guy?"

"His name is Dev," Aanya said, her voice soft. "He was in love with my grandmother. They planned to run away together, but they were caught. And then… he was taken away. She thought he was dead. She never spoke about him. Not to anyone."

Rohan's expression softened, and he nodded, handing the photograph back to her. "That must have been hard for her. And for you, finding all this out."

Aanya smiled faintly, tucking the photograph back into her bag. "It was. I just feel like there's so much I don't know about her. I want to see the place where she lived, where she loved. Maybe it will help me understand her better."

Rohan reached across the table and gave her hand a gentle squeeze. "You're doing a good thing, Aanya. I'm sure she'd be proud of you."

Aanya looked down at their hands, feeling a warmth spread through her chest. "Thank you, Rohan," she said, her voice barely a whisper.

Rohan smiled and then leaned back in his seat, looking out the window. "You know," he said, his tone thoughtful, "I think sometimes we have to go back to understand where we come from. It's like... if we don't understand our past, we can't really move forward."

Aanya nodded, his words resonating with her in a way she hadn't expected. She had always felt disconnected from her family's history, like she was floating without roots, without a foundation. Her grandmother had been her only link to that past, and now that she was gone, Aanya realised how much she needed to know, how much she needed to understand who her grandmother had been before she became the woman Aanya had known.

They spent the rest of the journey talking about mundane things: Rohan's work as a freelance photographer, the places he had travelled, and the people he had met. He spoke with a contagious enthusiasm, and Aanya found herself laughing more than she had in days. He showed her some of his photographs on his phone, images of bustling markets, quiet temples, and children playing by the riverside. His photographs had a way of capturing moments that were both ordinary and extraordinary, and Aanya found herself drawn to the way he saw the world.

"What about you?" Rohan asked, turning the conversation back to her. "What do you do?"

"I'm a writer," Aanya replied. "Freelance, mostly. Articles, short stories. I like to write about people, about their lives, their experiences."

Rohan raised an eyebrow, a smile tugging at his lips. "That makes sense. You're curious about your grandmother's story because you're a storyteller yourself."

Aanya smiled, considering his words. She had never thought of it that way, but maybe he was right. Maybe that was why she felt such a pull to uncover her grandmother's past – because it was a story that needed to be told, a story that had been lost to time, and Aanya was determined to bring it to life again.

She reached into her bag, pulling out the diary and flipping to a page she had already read countless times. The words seemed to glow in the dim light of the train car, and Aanya found herself reading and rereading them, Dadi's familiar script brimming with the same quiet intensity that never failed to draw her in.

"*15ᵗʰ August, 1952*

I know we must be careful. I know our love can never be here or like this. But in those moments under the banyan tree, I feel as though the world is ours, as though time itself has stopped, holding us in its gentle grasp. I think of Dev's laughter and his eyes… they hold a light that makes me feel alive, even in the darkest moments. I wish I could carry that light with me forever."

Aanya felt a tear slip down her cheek, her heart swelling with a longing that transcended words. This love, hidden and unspoken, was alive in every line, every whispered promise Dadi had poured onto these pages.

For a moment, she closed her eyes, letting the words sink in, feeling as though Dadi's memories had become her own. She could almost see the banyan tree, its twisted branches reaching out like arms, holding Dadi and Dev in their embrace. She imagined the village, with its winding paths and its quiet simplicity, and felt an undeniable urge to step into that world, to see it with her own eyes.

As the train continued on, Aanya knew that whatever lay ahead in Nandipur, she was ready. She would walk the paths Dadi had walked, listen to the whispers of the past, and carry forward the love that had survived in silence.

By the time they arrived in Varanasi the next morning, Aanya felt a sense of camaraderie with Rohan that she hadn't expected. The ancient city was waking up, the ghats bustling with pilgrims performing morning rituals, the aroma of incense thick in the air. The Ganges flowed beside them, its waters shimmering in the early morning light, and Aanya felt a sense of awe. There was something timeless about Varanasi, something sacred, and she wondered if her grandmother had ever been here if she had ever stood by the river and made a wish for a different life.

The taxi ride from Varanasi to Nandipur was long but scenic. The roads gradually narrowed, leaving behind the bustling city and winding through lush green fields and small hamlets. The air was cleaner and fresher, and Aanya rolled down the window, letting the wind blow her hair, savouring the freedom it brought. She closed her eyes, imagining her grandmother on this same journey, filled with hope, ready to defy the world for love.

Rohan seemed to sense her thoughts and remained quiet, snapping occasional pictures of the fields, the grazing cattle, and the schoolchildren walking alongside the road. The charm of rural life captivated him, and Aanya could see why. There was something raw, something undeniably real about this place.

As they approached Nandipur, Aanya's heartbeat quickened. The village was exactly how she had imagined it; it was picturesque and almost untouched by time. Mud houses with thatched roofs, children playing by the riverbank, women washing clothes, and old men sitting under banyan trees, puffing on their beedis, lost in conversation. Life here moved at a different pace, a slower, more deliberate rhythm, and Aanya felt herself being pulled into it.

"Welcome to Nandipur," Rohan said, smiling at her as he took her into the village.

Aanya nodded, her eyes scanning the scene, her heart pounding in her chest. There was something about this place that called to her a sense of belonging that she couldn't quite explain. She felt as though she had stepped into one of her grandmother's stories, the lines between past and present blurring until she could almost see her Dadi walking beside her. She imagined her grandmother, a young woman, laughing as she walked through these streets, her hand slipping into Dev's, their eyes filled with hope for a future that had never come to be.

Rohan stepped down beside her, his eyes sweeping over the scene with a mix of curiosity and thoughtfulness. He shifted the strap of his backpack on his shoulder, glancing at Aanya as if to gauge her reaction.

"So this is it," he said quietly, his voice cutting through the silence. "Nandipur. Hard to believe this tiny place holds so many of your Dadi's secrets."

Aanya nodded, unable to find the words. She was overwhelmed by the simplicity of it all, the faded colours, the unpaved streets, the soft hum of life unfolding at a pace far slower than anything she had ever known. It was almost like stepping into the past, each detail merging with the fragments she had pieced together from Dadi's diary.

Rohan touched her arm gently. "Are you okay?" he asked, his concern palpable.

"Yeah," she murmured, trying to steady her breath. "I just–it's surreal, you know? To finally be here, where Dadi lived and... loved."

He gave her a warm, reassuring smile. "One step at a time. We'll figure this out together."

They stood there for a moment longer, letting the silence settle around them. A small group of villagers passed by, throwing curious glances their way. The air was thick with the scent of earth and rain, mingled with something sweet and floral that Aanya couldn't quite place. It was sensory overload, and yet everything felt oddly familiar as if she had visited this place in her dreams.

They checked into a small guesthouse run by an elderly couple. The rooms were simple – wooden furniture, clean white sheets, and a window that looked out onto the fields.

It was perfect. The elderly woman, who introduced herself as Sharda, was kind, her eyes crinkling at the corners as she smiled at them.

As they stood in the cosy warmth of the guesthouse, a gentle breeze drifted in through the open window, carrying the faint scent of wildflowers and earth after the morning rain. Aanya's gaze lingered on the fields stretching beyond the village, golden under the soft sun, and she felt a strange sense of peace settle over her as if the place itself was welcoming them. Sharda's soft laughter from the kitchen filled the quiet, mingling with the distant sounds of the village, a cow's low moo, children's laughter, and the rhythmic thump of a potter's wheel nearby. It felt worlds away from Mumbai's hum, and for a moment, Aanya let herself sink into the simplicity around her, almost forgetting the purpose that had brought her here. Then, Rohan's voice broke through her thoughts, and she turned to him, her curiosity mingling with anticipation as she nodded towards the path, ready for whatever secrets the village might reveal.

"Where to first?" Rohan asked, breaking the silence. He adjusted his backpack and nodded towards the narrow road that led away from the station, winding its way into the heart of the village.

Aanya hesitated, then reached into her bag, pulling out the diary. She flipped through the pages until she found the entry describing Dadi's first meeting with Dev under the banyan tree. "The banyan tree at the temple," she said, her voice barely above a whisper. "Dadi wrote about it. It's where everything began."

Rohan's gaze flicked to the diary, then back to her face, understanding dawning in his eyes. "Alright, the temple it is," he agreed. "Lead the way."

They walked down the uneven cobblestone path, side by side, Aanya's mind racing with questions she hadn't dared to voice. What would they find here? Would the temple still look the way Dadi had described it? More importantly, would this journey give her the closure she was seeking or just open up more mysteries?

As they walked, Rohan tried to lighten the mood. "You know," he said, his tone playful, "if we're lucky, we might find one of those ancient villagers who knows everything about everyone. You know, the type who sits in the shade, just waiting to share some cryptic wisdom."

Aanya laughed softly, grateful for his attempt to ease her nerves. "Let's hope so. I could use some cryptic wisdom right about now."

He grinned, nudging her gently. "We've got this, Aanya. We're in it together, right?"

"Right," she agreed, feeling a wave of gratitude wash over her. It was comforting to have him here, his steady presence grounding her when everything else felt so uncertain.

The path twisted through the village, leading them past modest homes with brightly painted walls, their windows adorned with faded curtains fluttering in the gentle breeze. Children played barefoot in the streets, their laughter echoing off the worn brick walls. Aanya's eyes lingered on every detail, imagining Dadi as a young girl, running through these very same streets, her life full of dreams and possibilities that had since become whispers on the wind.

They turned a corner, and the temple came into view. It was small but beautifully constructed, its whitewashed walls standing out against the lush greenery that surrounded it. Intricate carvings of gods and goddesses decorated its pillars, worn down by years of sun and rain but still striking in their detail. Aanya stopped in her tracks, her heart racing as she took it all in. This was the place Dadi had written about a place where love had blossomed under the weight of tradition, where her grandmother had once dared to dream of a different life.

Rohan noticed her hesitation and stopped, too. "Is this it?" he asked, his voice soft.

She nodded, unable to speak. Her gaze fell upon a large banyan tree near the entrance, its roots twisting into the ground, its branches reaching out like arms that had held generations of stories. It was magnificent and ancient, a silent witness to the lives that had passed beneath its shade. A shiver ran down her spine as she realised this was the tree Dadi had written about.

They approached the tree slowly, Aanya's heart pounding in her chest. She reached out and placed her hand on its rough bark, feeling its warmth. It was as if she were touching a piece of history, a fragment of her grandmother's life brought back to the surface. She could almost see Dadi and Dev sitting beneath its shade, sharing whispered secrets, their love growing in the quiet spaces between words.

Rohan watched her, his expression thoughtful. "It's beautiful," he murmured. "You can feel the history here."

"Yeah," she replied, her voice choked with emotion. "This is where it all started."

They stood there in silence, the air thick with unspoken words. Aanya pulled the diary from her bag and turned to the entry that had led her there.

"August 20, 1952," she read aloud, her voice barely more than a whisper.

"Today, Dev and I met under the banyan tree at the temple. It felt as though the world had paused, as though this moment was carved out just for us. He spoke of dreams, not of leaving, but of building a life together in the haveli on the outskirts of the village. He said it could be our sanctuary, a place where we could create our own world, away from the judgements and constraints of others. His eyes lit up as he described it, and for a moment, I let myself believe it could be true."

She closed the diary, tears welling in her eyes. "She wanted so much more than she had," she whispered. "But she was afraid. Afraid to leave, afraid to lose what she knew."

Rohan placed a hand on her shoulder, his touch warm and reassuring. "It sounds like she was torn between two worlds," he said softly. "The life she was expected to live, and the life she wanted with him."

Aanya nodded, wiping away a tear. "I can't imagine what that must have felt like, loving someone so much but knowing it could never be."

They lingered beneath the banyan tree, the air around them heavy with the weight of history and untold stories. Aanya could feel Dadi's presence here, as if she were standing right beside her, urging her to uncover the truth, to finally bring to light the love that had been hidden for so long.

"We should probably keep moving," Rohan said gently, breaking the silence. "See what else we can find."

"Yeah," she agreed, slipping the diary back into her bag. "But I want to come back here before we leave. I feel like... there's something more."

He nodded. "We'll come back. I promise."

As they walked away, Aanya glanced back at the tree one last time, a sense of resolve settling over her. She was ready to face whatever lay ahead, to piece together the fragments of Dadi's life, no matter how painful or complicated it might be. With Rohan by her side and the diary as her guide, she knew she could handle whatever Nandipur had in store.

This was just the beginning.

Keeper of the Forgotten Tales

The soft crunch of gravel underfoot echoed in the stillness as Aanya and Rohan approached the small, weathered house tucked beneath the shade of an ancient neem tree. Chandrika Devi's home, they had been told, was one of the oldest in the village, a place of stories and whispered legends. The modest house, with its clay walls and faded turquoise paint, seemed to hold its own quiet wisdom, the kind that ages slowly with time and solitude.

Aanya glanced at Rohan, her thoughts racing as they neared their destination. Her heartbeat quickened at the thought of the woman they were about to meet – a woman who had known her grandmother in a way perhaps no one else had, someone who possibly held the missing pieces to complete the story of Dadi's life.

They stopped at the entrance, and Aanya hesitated before calling out, "Namaste, Chandrika Devi?"

A moment passed, and then the door opened. A woman, silver-haired and sharp-eyed, appeared in the doorway, her gaze settling on Aanya with a quiet intensity. She wore a faded cotton sari, its edges worn from years of wear, and her face held the gentle creases of someone who had lived a life filled with both love and loss.

"You must be Savitri's granddaughter," Chandrika Devi said, her voice soft but clear, as though she had known Aanya her whole life. "I see so much of her in you."

Aanya felt a lump in her throat as she nodded. "Yes, I am. I came to learn more about her... and about Dev."

Chandrika Devi's eyes softened, a faint, bittersweet smile tracing her lips. She stepped aside, gesturing them in. "Then you've come to the right place. There are things you need to know, stories she entrusted to me, stories that were never meant to be forgotten."

Aanya exchanged a look with Rohan before stepping inside. The air was filled with a blend of incense and age-old spices, and everywhere she looked, relics of the past surrounded her, paintings, rusted lanterns, small idols of gods and goddesses, and books stacked neatly along the walls. It was as if she had stepped into another time, into a sanctuary where her grandmother's life had left a lasting impression.

Aanya followed her inside, her heart thudding with a strange blend of nervousness and reverence.

As Aanya looked around, her eyes were drawn to a narrow shelf where brass oil lamps cast a soft glow over a faded photograph of Dadi. Aanya's breath caught as she gazed at her grandmother's face, youthful and filled with a joy that seemed almost ethereal. It was the same photograph she had seen in Dadi's old home, yet here, within these walls, it felt more alive, more meaningful.

Chandrika noticed Aanya's lingering gaze and smiled gently. "Savitri was like the younger sister I never had," she said softly, her voice carrying the warmth of fond memories. "As toddlers, she and her friend Lakshmi used to shadow me wherever I went, always trying to copy me. But as they grew older, they would come to me with their sorrows or seek my guidance, trusting me with their hearts in a way that made our bond even stronger."

Aanya's throat tightened as she took in Chandrika's words. "I never knew how much she kept hidden," she admitted. "Her diary is full of things she never spoke about, not even to my mother. Things about... Dev."

At the mention of his name, a shadow of remembrance flickered across Chandrika's face. She gestured for them to sit, lowering herself onto a cushion opposite Aanya. "Dev," she murmured, her voice softened by the tenderness of old memories. "That name was a balm to her heart. He was the one who gave her courage, who made her feel alive in ways the world would not permit. They met in secret beneath the banyan tree at the temple. That tree became a sanctuary for them, a place untouched by judgement or duty."

Rohan leaned forward, his gaze intent. "Why did they have to hide their love?"

Chandrika's eyes shifted to him, her expression tinged with sadness. "In those days, a woman's life was bound to the expectations of her family. Love, as we know it, was not a luxury all could afford. Savitri and Dev came from different worlds; their love was like a fire, fierce but forbidden." She turned back to Aanya, her gaze tender. "Your Dadi was brave, child. She dared to hope, even when it felt like a futile dream."

Aanya clutched the diary tighter, feeling the silent weight of her grandmother's unspoken desires. "Did she ever regret it?" she whispered. "Did she ever wish she had chosen differently?"

Chandrika's gaze softened, her voice gentle yet firm. "No, Aanya. She loved Dev with a depth and purity that few understood. To love him, even briefly, was to live a thousand lifetimes in a single moment. And that love, however hidden, never left her." She paused, her gaze shifting to the window as if seeing her friend there, smiling in memory only she could see. "Though she carried that love like a secret flame, it was also a source of strength. She may have accepted a different path, but she never let go of the memory of what could have been."

Aanya's eyes brimmed with tears, and she felt Rohan's hand rest gently on her shoulder, a steady presence amid her swirling emotions. She thought of Dadi, carrying a love so profound yet locked away from the world, a love that had shaped her even as she moved forward with quiet grace. "She must have been so lonely," Aanya murmured, her voice thick with the weight of unspoken sorrow. "To hold that love alone, without anyone to share it with."

Chandrika reached out, covering Aanya's hand with her own. "She may have been alone, but she was never without love. Dev's memory stayed with her, a silent companion through the years. And now, she has given that memory to you to honour and understand."

As the words settled over them, Chandrika rose and walked to a small chest in the corner of the room, unlocking it with a brass key that hung around her neck. She lifted the lid with a reverence that spoke of years spent guarding a treasure. From within, she drew out a delicate, faded letter and returned it to Aanya, placing it gently in her hands.

"Your Dadi left this with me before she departed from Nandipur," Chandrika said, her voice soft but steady. "She told me to keep it safe in case someone came looking for Dev for her story. I believe this was meant for you."

Aanya unfolded the letter with trembling hands, the fragile paper bearing the faint scent of jasmine and sandalwood. She read the first line, her grandmother's handwriting sweeping across the page like the gentle strokes of a paintbrush.

"*My beloved Dev,*" the letter began, "*though we may walk separate paths, know that my heart will always carry the memory of our love as bright as the stars above Nandipur. In each breath, in each quiet moment, you are with me…*"

Aanya's heart broke open as she read, tears slipping down her cheeks. These words, once held in silence, now resonated like a haunting melody, binding her to her grandmother's past in ways she could barely comprehend. She felt Rohan's hand tighten around her shoulder, his quiet strength anchoring her as the weight of her grandmother's love and loss settled within her.

Chandrika watched her with an understanding gaze. "She wanted you to know, Aanya. She wanted you to feel the love that shaped her life, that gave her the courage to carry on. And she entrusted you with her story, knowing that you would carry it forward."

Aanya closed her eyes, pressing the letter to her chest. In that moment, she felt the spirit of her grandmother beside her, a warm, invisible presence that soothed her grief and strengthened her resolve. "Thank you," she whispered, her voice barely audible, "for keeping this, for protecting her memory."

Chandrika's eyes glistened with unshed tears as she patted Aanya's hand. "Your grandmother was a rare soul. She carried her love like a quiet ember, hidden but never extinguished. And now, it is yours to carry, to honour in whatever way you choose."

They sat together in silence, a shared understanding thickening the air between them. The late afternoon sun cast long shadows across the room, gilding the edges of the worn furniture and illuminating the dust motes suspended in the golden light. The silence was rich with unspoken words, memories layered over the years like the patina on the brass ornaments lining the shelves. It was as if the light itself acknowledged the presence of love that had endured in the silences, persisting even when words had failed to hold it.

After a long pause, Chandrika spoke again, her voice gentle yet resolute. "There is one more thing I can share with you, Aanya. A place that was sacred to your grandmother. It was where she and Dev spent their last moments together. It lies on the outskirts of the village, near the river. When you're ready, I will show you the way."

Aanya looked at her, a mixture of gratitude and sorrow filling her chest. She nodded, feeling a sense of purpose settle within her. This was more than a journey through her grandmother's past; it was a journey to understand her own soul, to connect with the woman whose legacy she had inherited. "I want to go there," she said softly. "To see the place where she loved him, where she let him go."

Chandrika smiled, her eyes filled with gentle wisdom. "Then we will go together."

As they prepared to leave, Aanya felt the diary in her bag, a sacred testament to a love that had transcended time, bound by silence and now finally spoken through her. She glanced at Rohan, who met her gaze with a quiet understanding, his presence a source of strength as she prepared to take the next steps.

The sun had dipped lower in the sky as they left Chandrika's home, casting long shadows across the narrow village streets. Aanya felt a profound sense of calm settle over her, a feeling that came not from ease but from purpose. The letter, carefully folded and pressed close to her heart, felt like a bridge between past and present, a connection to the woman her grandmother had been before she became 'Dadi'.

Chandrika led them along a path winding through the village, the air rich with the scent of evening jasmine and wood smoke curling up from nearby homes. The streets had quieted, leaving only the sounds of footsteps and the gentle hum of crickets filling the space around them. Rohan walked beside Aanya, a steady, silent support as she absorbed each moment, each detail of this village that had cradled her grandmother's heart.

As they neared the river, the landscape opened into an expanse of wild grass and flowering shrubs. The river stretched out before them, its waters shimmering with the soft, fading light. A small, weathered bench stood beneath a canopy of trees, overlooking the water, a simple spot, yet one filled with an ineffable beauty. Aanya felt an inexplicable pull towards it, her heart beating with the pulse of unspoken memories.

"This is where she would come," Chandrika said, her voice barely more than a whisper. "When things became too heavy when the weight of her love and its impossibility threatened to break her, she would sit here and let the river carry her burdens away."

Aanya's eyes stung with tears as she walked towards the bench, her fingers tracing its worn wooden edges. She could almost see Dadi here, young and hopeful, her heart alive with dreams of a future that would never be. She pictured her sitting in this very spot, gazing out at the river with thoughts of Dev, her love for him an unbreakable thread woven through the fabric of her life.

She sat down slowly, letting the quiet of the place wrap around her. Rohan settled beside her, his presence grounding her as if sensing that words were unnecessary. Chandrika stood a few steps away, giving Aanya the space she needed, her eyes filled with a tender understanding.

Aanya reached for Dadi's diary in her bag, flipping through the pages until she found an entry that described this very place:

"There is a place by the river, a quiet sanctuary where I feel close to him, even when he's not there. The waters carry my secrets, the wind my hopes. It is here that I come to remember, to remember who I am and who I once dared to be."

Aanya closed her eyes, letting the words settle in her heart, her grandmother's voice a soft murmur within her. The love Dadi had carried, even in silence, had left an indelible mark, a love that had transcended time, defying the boundaries imposed by tradition and loss.

When she opened her eyes, Rohan was watching her, his gaze filled with quiet empathy. He reached out, placing his hand over hers, his warmth steady and reassuring.

"You're carrying her story forward," he said softly, his voice like a balm. "By being here, by remembering... you're giving her love a voice."

As the light began to fade, Chandrika approached. Her steps were quiet, and she joined them by the riverbank. She held out a small, ornate pendant, a single stone glinting softly in the twilight.

"Your Dadi left this with me," she said, placing it gently in Aanya's palm. "It was a gift from Dev, a symbol of their love. She wore it close to her heart, even after they could no longer be together."

Aanya turned the pendant over in her hand, her thumb tracing the delicate, intricate design. She felt the weight of its history, the love it symbolised, and she closed her hand around it, feeling an overwhelming connection to Dadi, to the life she had led with courage and grace.

"Thank you," Aanya whispered, her voice thick with emotion. "For everything... for keeping her memories alive."

Chandrika smiled, her eyes glistening with the wisdom of a lifetime. "Some stories are meant to live on, Aanya. Your Dadi's love was one of them. She lived quietly, but her heart was fierce. And now, that heart lives on in you."

As the last traces of sunlight slipped below the horizon, Aanya felt a peace settle over her, a quiet assurance that Dadi's love, though hidden and unspoken, had found a way to endure. She glanced at Rohan, his face softened in the dusk, his expression thoughtful.

Rohan turned to her, his voice a gentle murmur. "Are you ready to continue, Aanya? To see the other places she wrote about, to uncover the rest of her story?"

Aanya nodded, a small, resolute smile tugging at her lips. "Yes," she replied, her voice steady. "This journey... it's no longer just about her. It's about understanding the legacy of love she has passed down to me."

They stood together in the fading light; the pendant clasped in Aanya's hand like a talisman, a link to the woman whose love had become an unbreakable thread woven into the fabric of her own heart. As they turned to leave, the river behind them carried the echoes of the past, and Aanya knew that her grandmother's story was only beginning to be told.

Seeking Silent Witnesses

S oft morning light filtered through the small windows
of the guesthouse dining area, casting a warm glow
over the modest spread on the table. Aanya and Rohan
sat cross-legged on the floor, savouring the aroma of freshly
made parathas and steaming cups of chai. The quiet hum
of the village was just starting to drift in through the open
window, cows lowing, children's laughter, the faint sound
of a distant temple bell.

Sharda moved gracefully around the kitchen,
humming a tune under her breath as she placed a bowl
of spiced yoghurt and a plate of pickles in front of them.
Her weathered hands, steady and practised, spoke of years
spent in the rhythm of village life, a life untouched by the
hurried pace of the world beyond Nandipur.

"So," Sharda said, settling herself on a small stool
near them with a knowing look in her eye. "I sense you

didn't come all the way here just to see temples and banyan trees, did you?"

Aanya hesitated, glancing at Rohan before replying. "I came here because of my grandmother. She grew up here, and... well, she left behind stories that were never told. I want to understand her better, to see the places that were once a part of her life."

Sharda nodded thoughtfully, her gaze softening as she poured more tea into their cups. "Savitri Sharma, wasn't it? I remember her faintly from when I was young. She had a presence, your grandmother, quiet but strong."

Aanya leaned forward, her voice filled with anticipation. "Did you know her?"

"Only in passing," Sharda replied, her tone almost wistful. "But there's someone who did–Lakshmi Kaki. She was one of Savitri's closest friends when they were young. If anyone can tell you about the life your grandmother led here, it would be her."

Aanya nodded, a flicker of recognition crossing her face. "Chandrika Aunty mentioned her friend Lakshmi," she said, her tone thoughtful. "We were so overwhelmed with everything she told us, we never got around to asking more about her. Can you tell us where we might find her?"

Rohan leaned in slightly, his curiosity mirroring Aanya's. "It sounds like she could help us piece this together," he added.

Sharda smiled, a glint of amusement in her eyes as though she'd anticipated their interest. "Lakshmi Kaki lives just a short walk away, under the biggest mango tree in the village. Her house is easy to spot, with turquoise walls and a roof that looks as if it's seen every monsoon since time began. She keeps to herself these days, but she has a mind like a lockbox. If she decides to open up, you'll hear stories you never imagined."

Aanya felt a thrill of anticipation, her hand instinctively brushing the diary tucked into her bag. "Thank you, Sharda ji," she said softly, her gratitude evident.

Sharda nodded, her expression turning thoughtful as she looked out of the window, her gaze distant. "There's something you should know about Lakshmi Kaki; she's a woman who values loyalty and doesn't speak lightly of the past. But if she chooses to share, you'll be hearing the truth, for better or worse."

With that, Sharda stood and gathered the empty plates, her hands lingering over the table's worn wood.

After finishing their breakfast, Aanya and Rohan made their way outside, the cool morning air carrying with it the faint scents of jasmine and damp earth. The village, with its ancient trees and simple charm, felt timeless, almost as if it held secrets woven into every leaf and stone.

With Sharda's words still lingering in her mind, Aanya followed the narrow path with Rohan beside her, both of them ready to step further into her grandmother's world.

Their destination, Lakshmi Kaki's house, stood tucked away beneath a massive mango tree, its branches heavy with fruit that dangled like small lanterns in the soft morning light. The house was humble, a low structure with faded turquoise walls and a thatched roof, each detail softened by time and the elements. Aanya's heart thrummed with anticipation, her fingers absentmindedly grazing the leather cover of Dadi's diary in her bag. Chandrika had spoken of Lakshmi Kaki as a woman of great wisdom, a keeper of stories and secrets, someone who had known her grandmother before she became the reserved, dignified figure Aanya remembered.

As they reached the gate, Rohan cast a glance her way, his expression gentle and reassuring. They exchanged a silent nod, and then he knocked gently on the door, his knuckles tapping against the worn wood in a respectful rhythm.

Moments later, the door opened, revealing Lakshmi Kaki, her figure framed by the soft light spilling in from the window behind her. She was an elderly woman, small and slightly stooped, but her presence radiated strength and dignity that made Aanya feel as though she were in the presence of someone ancient and wise. Her hair, streaked with silver, was gathered in a loose braid that trailed over one shoulder, and her eyes—clear and penetrating—studied Aanya with a warmth that felt instantly familiar.

"You are Savitri's granddaughter," she said, her voice a low, steady murmur, filled with the quiet certainty of someone who had long awaited this moment. There was no surprise in her tone, only a soft, knowing acceptance, as if Aanya's arrival had been foretold.

"Yes, I am," Aanya replied, her voice barely above a whisper. "My name is Aanya. And this is Rohan." She gestured to her friend, who offered a respectful nod.

Lakshmi Kaki's face softened into a gentle smile, her eyes crinkling at the edges as she motioned them inside. "Come, come. You've travelled a long way, and you must be tired." Her voice was warm, inviting, like the crackle of a fire on a cold night.

Inside, the house was filled with the fragrance of sandalwood and dried herbs, mingling with the scent of freshly brewed tea. The walls were adorned with woven tapestries, their colours faded but still vibrant with intricate patterns of flowers and birds. A single brass oil lamp flickered on a low table, casting soft, golden shadows that danced across the room. There was a stillness here, a reverent calm that made Aanya feel as though she had stepped into a place where time moved more slowly, where stories lingered in the air like an unbroken song.

Lakshmi Kaki settled onto a low stool by the window, gesturing for Aanya and Rohan to sit on the woven mat spread across the floor. She studied Aanya with an intensity that was both comforting and unsettling, as though she were looking not at her face but into the very fabric of her soul.

"You have her eyes," she said softly, almost to herself. "Savitri was a dreamer, too—a woman who carried the weight of a love too fierce to fit within the boundaries of our world."

Aanya felt a lump rise in her throat, her hands tightening around the diary in her lap. "Did you know her well?" she asked, her voice tinged with desperation she hadn't meant to reveal.

Lakshmi Kaki nodded, her expression distant, her gaze lost in memories. "I knew her from the time she was a little girl. She had a light in her, a fire that could not be tamed. And then... then she met Dev. The two of them were like the earth and the rai, different, yet drawn to each other by a force beyond their control." She paused, her voice softening. "Their love was beautiful, but it was also a heavy burden. In those days, a woman's life was not her own; it belonged to her family, to tradition, to the expectations of our village."

Aanya leaned forward, captivated, feeling the weight of her grandmother's story settle over her like a shawl woven with sorrow and love. "They met under the banyan tree, didn't they?" she asked, her voice barely above a whisper. "Chandrika told us it was their place, a sanctuary where they could be together."

Lakshmi Kaki's eyes gleamed with a spark of mystery. "Ah, the banyan tree... Yes, that tree holds many secrets. But it is no ordinary tree, Aanya. There is a legend about it, a story as old as the village itself."

Rohan's gaze flicked to Aanya, his expression intrigued. "What kind of legend?" he asked, leaning in as though he, too, could feel the pull of the mystery Lakshmi Kaki was about to reveal.

Lakshmi Kaki's voice dropped to a reverent murmur, her tone weaving the tale like a spell. "The banyan tree has stood for generations, its roots winding deep into the earth, binding it to the spirits of those who have loved and lost beneath its branches. It is said that the tree holds the memories of all who have whispered their secrets within its shade, that it remembers every laugh, every tear, every promise."

Aanya's breath caught, her heart beating faster as she listened. The idea that the tree might hold echoes of her grandmother's voice, that it might have witnessed the love Dadi and Dev shared, filled her with a sense of awe and longing.

Lakshmi Kaki leaned closer, her gaze piercing. "They say that if two souls are bound by love, true love, the tree protects their bond. Even when the world separates them, the tree guards their connection, keeping it alive, preserved in its roots, its branches, its leaves. If you sit beneath that tree and listen with an open heart, you may hear the whispers of those who came before, their voices carried on the wind."

Aanya felt a shiver run through her, a mixture of awe and fear. She could almost see her grandmother and Dev beneath that tree, their hands entwined, their love hidden but unbroken. "Do you think… that the tree still remembers them?" she asked, her voice thick with emotion.

Lakshmi Kaki's gaze softened; her eyes filled with a tender understanding. "Oh, child, the tree remembers. Your Dadi's spirit lingers there, I'm sure of it. She left a piece of herself within those roots, a part of her love for Dev that could not be taken away. If you sit beneath its branches and let yourself listen, truly listen, perhaps you will hear the truth you seek."

Rohan glanced at Aanya, his expression a mixture of wonder and encouragement. "Aanya, this is incredible… Maybe this is what you came here for, to uncover what the tree has kept hidden all these years."

Lakshmi Kaki nodded, her gaze never leaving Aanya's face. "But remember, child," she cautioned, her voice deepening with a solemn warning. "The banyan tree does not reveal its secrets easily. It is a guardian, a keeper of stories, and it only shares them with those who are prepared to bear their weight. The truths it holds are not always easy to accept."

Aanya's heart pounded in her chest, her emotions a tangled web of curiosity, fear, and longing. She thought of Dadi's diary, the words etched in love and sorrow, and the unspoken story that had brought her all this way. "I don't know if I'm ready," she admitted, her voice trembling. "But I have to try. I need to know her story. I need to understand her."

Lakshmi Kaki reached out, her weathered hand closing over Aanya's. "You carry her strength within you, Aanya. The tree will recognise that. Go to it with an open heart, and let the spirits guide you. They may reveal the truth, not only of your grandmother's love, but of the legacy she left for you."

Aanya nodded, feeling a surge of gratitude for Lakshmi Kaki's wisdom. This woman, with her deep knowledge and quiet strength, had given her more than guidance; she had given her the courage to face the unknown.

As they prepared to leave, Lakshmi Kaki rose and moved to a small wooden shelf, pulling down a tiny, handwoven pouch. She pressed it into Aanya's hand, her gaze soft but resolute. "Inside is a petal from the marigolds that grow near the banyan tree. They are said to carry blessings, a protection from those who came before. Keep it with you, child, as you go on your journey."

Aanya held the pouch to her chest, feeling its warmth seep into her heart. "Thank you, Lakshmi Kaki," she whispered, her voice filled with reverence. "For your guidance and for your kindness."

Lakshmi Kaki smiled, her eyes filled with gentle wisdom. "Go, child. The banyan tree awaits. It has kept its secrets long enough, and it will know when you are ready to hear them."

As Aanya and Rohan stepped back into the morning light, Aanya felt a quiet determination settle within her, as if a path she had not known was there had suddenly opened before her. The banyan tree, that silent keeper of stories, awaited her. And with each step she took, she felt closer not only to Dadi's love but to the deepest parts of her own heart.

Rohan looked at her, his expression one of understanding and encouragement. "Are you ready?"

Aanya nodded, her hand closing around the small pouch Lakshmi Kaki had given her, a talisman that felt like a bridge to her grandmother's past. "As ready as I'll ever be."

They walked side by side towards the heart of Nandipur, where the banyan tree stood as it had for generations. As they drew closer, Aanya felt as though the air itself was holding its breath, the world waiting for her to uncover the love that had been whispered into the roots, waiting to be heard once again.

The Ghosts of a Forgotten Love

The morning sun was now fully awake, casting its golden light over Nandipur as Aanya and Rohan left Lakshmi Kaki's house. Each step they took was accompanied by a quiet sense of purpose, an awareness of the journey they were about to undertake. The little pouch with the marigold petal rested snugly in Aanya's hand, and she clutched it like a precious link to her grandmother's past, a small but potent blessing from someone who had understood the weight of the story she was trying to uncover.

Rohan walked beside her, his presence steady and reassuring, and as they rounded the curve of the narrow village path, he glanced over, sensing her emotions. "Lakshmi Kaki really believes the tree holds a part of your grandmother," he murmured, a note of awe in his voice. "It's like something out of one of your stories."

Aanya smiled faintly, her heart heavy yet filled with anticipation. "This feels more real than any story I could ever write," she replied, her gaze fixed on the distant form of the banyan tree, its branches spread wide as if embracing the sky. "It's like... I'm not just hearing Dadi's story but stepping into it, breathing it."

As they walked, the village seemed to quiet around them, the gentle sounds of daily life—murmured conversations, the clink of pots, the laughter of children—fading into the background. The banyan tree loomed larger with every step, its roots snaking across the ground in ancient patterns as if marking the passage of time. Aanya felt a slight tremor in her hands as she approached and paused just short of the tree's shade, gathering herself for what lay ahead.

"This is where she felt free," she whispered, almost to herself. "The one place where she could be with him, where her love wasn't hidden away."

Rohan placed a comforting hand on her shoulder. "Take your time," he said softly. "We're here, and there's no rush."

Aanya took a deep breath, then stepped beneath the sprawling canopy of the banyan tree. The air was calm, grounding her in an unexpected way. Aanya stood beneath the tree, its towering presence a quiet reminder of the lives and stories that had unfolded around it, shaping her path to this moment.

Sitting down on the soft earth, she gently opened the pouch Lakshmi Kaki had given her, letting the marigold petal rest in her palm as she closed her eyes. For a moment, she allowed herself to imagine her grandmother sitting here, the young Savitri, her heart full of dreams, laughing with Dev in a world that was just theirs.

The wind stirred, rustling the leaves above them, and in that quiet murmur, Aanya could almost hear the echoes of past conversations, of promises made under the shelter of the banyan tree. She felt her grandmother's presence in a way she hadn't felt before, a closeness that brought both comfort and sorrow.

A tear slipped down her cheek, and she opened her eyes, looking up at Rohan, who watched her with quiet understanding. "Maybe Lakshmi Kaki was right," she whispered. "Maybe this tree does remember."

Rohan nodded, his gaze shifting from Aanya's tear-streaked face to the massive roots and branches that seemed to cradle them in their quiet strength. "It feels alive with memory," he said, almost in awe. "As if it's been holding on to the love, the secrets, the sorrows of everyone who's come here."

Aanya's fingers grazed the marigold petal in her palm, its vivid orange contrasting sharply against the earthy tones around her. She placed the petal on the ground, near the tree's roots, feeling as though she were offering something small but significant, a piece of herself, perhaps, to the history held in the tree's embrace. She ran her fingers along the rough bark, feeling its grooves and ridges, each line a testament to years of silent witness.

Just then, a soft breeze swept through, stirring the air, and from the corner of her eye, she noticed something remarkable: scattered across the roots, nestled among the dirt and moss, were clusters of marigold flowers, vibrant and delicate. The petals seemed freshly fallen, their fragrance mingling with the earthy scent of the tree, creating an aroma that was both grounding and ethereal.

"Rohan," she breathed, motioning to the flowers. "Look... the marigolds. Just like Lakshmi Kaki said."

Rohan knelt beside her, his expression one of astonishment. "They're beautiful. It's as if they're... part of the tree's story."

Aanya picked up a marigold, cradling it gently in her palm. The flower felt warm, alive, as if it carried the energy of the past, of her grandmother's laughter, of Dev's quiet promises, of love that had lived and lingered despite the constraints that surrounded it. She closed her eyes, inhaling deeply, letting herself fall deeper into her grandmother's story, imagining the young Savitri sitting in this very spot, her heart filled with a love that was both a gift and a burden.

Aanya took a deep breath, her eyes drifting over the expansive roots that seemed to breathe with a life of their own. She felt a gentle but undeniable pull, as if she were being welcomed into a sacred space that had been waiting for her. She dropped her bag to the ground and let her fingers trail over the bark, rough and cool beneath her touch, and sat down at the base of the tree.

Rohan settled nearby, his gaze lingering on her with a quiet understanding as she pulled out her notebook. She opened her notebook, feeling a strange calmness settle over her as she began writing, letting words spill onto the page. She wrote of her grandmother, the hidden love she'd found in the old diary, and the weight of secrets carried across generations. Her pen moved quickly, capturing the story that had begun to emerge in Nandipur.

Meanwhile, Rohan leaned against the tree's trunk, glancing through the letters, journals, and diary entries they had uncovered so far. Each word revealed fragments of Savitri's past, moments of her youth and family life in Nandipur that shaped her. He lingered on her descriptions of the childhood house, a sanctuary where she'd first dreamed of a life beyond the village walls. He could almost see the old home, its turquoise walls softened by sun and rain, its worn stones bearing the imprints of laughter and tears.

As he continued reading, he found out more about the haveli in the diary entries or letters, a place that Savitri had described as both grand and intimidating. It was the heart of her family's legacy, its rooms filled with relics of another era, each one a reminder of the traditions she was expected to uphold. Her words painted the haveli as a place of both pride and confinement, a place where duty often overshadowed desire.

Rohan looked up at Aanya, who was immersed in her writing, her brow furrowed in concentration. "You know," he said softly, breaking the quiet, "it's amazing how much of her life you're piecing together. Every letter, every memory... it's like you're weaving her story back together, thread by thread."

Aanya looked up from her notebook, a faint smile on her lips. "It feels like I'm not just discovering her story," she murmured. "It feels like I'm discovering a part of myself, too. There's so much in these places, in this village, that makes me feel connected to her in ways I never expected."

Rohan nodded, his gaze shifting to the marigold flowers that lay scattered near the tree's roots. Their vibrant orange petals seemed to glow against the earthy ground, a startling contrast that felt almost intentional. "Look," he said, motioning to the flowers. "The marigolds. Just like Lakshmi Kaki mentioned."

Aanya followed his gaze, her heart swelling as she reached out to touch one of the blossoms. It was soft and warm, its scent rich and familiar. She felt a sense of gratitude as she tucked a marigold into her notebook, a small tribute to the life her grandmother had lived and the love she had cherished beneath this tree.

They sat there for a while, wrapped in the quiet presence of the banyan tree, the marigold petals, and the lingering memories. As they prepared to leave, Aanya felt a renewed determination.

Aanya took one last look at the banyan tree, its branches arching over them like a shelter. She tucked her notebook back into her bag, feeling a sense of accomplishment but also an aching anticipation for what she might uncover next. Standing up, she brushed the earth from her clothes and glanced at Rohan, who was still holding the last of her grandmother's letters.

"Ready?" he asked, offering her a gentle smile.

She nodded, feeling a swell of gratitude for his presence. "More than ready."

They walked back along the village path, and the morning sounds began to stir around them again. Aanya couldn't help but feel the tree's presence lingering with her; its quiet, almost watchful energy was a reminder that she had only just scratched the surface of the story she was discovering.

As they reached the guesthouse, Aanya's thoughts drifted back to her grandmother's childhood home and the haveli. Her grandmother's words, vivid in her letters, described the haveli as a place brimming with expectations and traditions—its halls filled with an unspoken authority that weighed heavily on her dreams. In contrast, her childhood home had been a place of innocence and wonder, where she'd first felt the stirrings of freedom, a stark contrast to the life that would later be shaped by family obligations and duty.

They settled on the veranda, overlooking the courtyard where village life bustled. Rohan sat cross-legged with a stack of letters in front of him. He picked up one and began reading aloud, his voice low and steady, bringing the words to life as if conjuring Savitri's voice.

In one letter, Savitri wrote about her first years in the haveli after marrying Rajesh, a young man chosen by her family. She described the grand rooms, the imposing portraits of ancestors watching her every move, and the sprawling courtyards that felt too vast, too cold. Her words carried a deep melancholy, tinged with longing for the simpler, open spaces of her childhood home. It was here, she admitted, that she'd truly felt the loss of Dev, the life she'd almost had.

Aanya leaned back, her heart heavy. "I wonder if she ever stopped loving him," she whispered, more to herself than to Rohan. "Even when she moved into the haveli and built a life with someone else."

Rohan set down the letter, his gaze thoughtful. "Maybe love doesn't just disappear. Maybe it becomes something else, something quieter but no less powerful. And in a way, her life at the haveli would have always held his memory."

Aanya absorbed his words, feeling a shiver pass through her. The depth of her grandmother's love—and the sacrifices she'd made—was almost overwhelming. To imagine living in a place so bound by tradition, with Dev's memory hidden deep within her heart, was something she couldn't fully fathom.

Rohan thumbed through another letter, his brow furrowing as he read. "This one mentions the banyan tree again," he said, intrigued. "She writes about visiting it after marrying Rajesh. She said it was like visiting an old friend, someone who kept her secrets safe even when she had to lock them away in her own heart."

Aanya's breath caught. "So even after she had built a life apart from Dev, she would still go back to the tree–to that part of herself that loved him."

They sat in silence for a long moment, the weight of the letters pressing on them. Aanya felt as though each word had lifted another veil from her grandmother's life, revealing the hidden layers that had been lost to time. She closed her eyes, feeling closer to her grandmother than she ever had, as though she too had inherited the quiet strength that had allowed Savitri to carry her love forward, even in silence.

Finally, Aanya took a deep breath and stood. "I want to go to the haveli," she said, her voice filled with resolve. "I need to see where she lived, the place she called home after she left everything behind."

Rohan looked at her, his expression supportive and steady. "Then let's go tomorrow. We're here to see this through together, remember?"

With one last look at the letters, Aanya placed them carefully back in her bag, knowing they would guide her through the halls of the haveli and whatever memories lingered within its walls. She felt ready to confront the truths her grandmother had lived, both the joy and the sorrow, in the hopes of understanding the legacy she now carried.

The Silent Remnants

The morning unfurled over Nandipur with a kind of reverence, a hushed awakening that seemed to resonate with the secrets Aanya was on the verge of uncovering. The light spread slowly, casting a delicate wash over the village that softened every edge, bathing it in a glow that seemed almost magical. In the early haze, she felt as though she were walking in a world halfway between memory and reality, a world her grandmother, Savitri, had once known as her own.

Rohan walked beside her, matching her quiet steps, his face thoughtful as he absorbed the ambiance of this village that had been such an essential part of her family's past. His presence was grounding, and she felt a wave of gratitude for his silent understanding, for his willingness to accompany her on this deeply personal journey. With each step, she felt as if she were moving closer to the heart of her grandmother's story, peeling back layers of time.

Their first stop was Savitri's childhood home, a modest two-storey house set just off the main path, nestled beneath the shade of an ancient neem tree. The once-bright blue walls had faded to a gentle teal, softened by years of monsoons, sunlight, and the quiet passage of time. Vines clung to its sides like gentle hands, their tendrils weaving a delicate latticework up toward the tiled roof. It was a place that seemed to hold its own memories, a silent guardian of the life it had once sheltered.

Aanya paused at the small iron gate, now rusted and overgrown with wild jasmine, its pale flowers releasing a scent so light, so ethereal, it felt like the memory of a fragrance rather than something real. She pushed the gate open, and it groaned in protest, a sound that echoed through the stillness like the sigh of something long forgotten. She took a deep breath and stepped into the courtyard, her gaze sweeping over the stones that had been worn smooth by countless footsteps.

The courtyard was overgrown now, patches of wildflowers and weeds bursting through the cobblestones. She could almost see her grandmother as a young girl, running barefoot over these stones, her laughter ringing out in the morning air. Aanya closed her eyes for a moment, letting herself sink into the image of Savitri, untouched by the world's expectations, her heart as open as the sky. It was a version of her grandmother she'd never known, but in this space, she felt close to her, almost as if she could reach out and hold her hand.

"It's beautiful," Rohan murmured beside her, his voice a soft breath, as if afraid to shatter the spell of the morning. "It feels like... it's waiting to be remembered."

Aanya nodded, unable to speak. Her throat felt tight, and a wave of emotion rose within her as she stepped towards the front door. She pushed it open slowly, the wood cool beneath her hand, and they stepped inside, entering a world held in quiet stasis.

The interior was dim, the air thick with the scent of sandalwood and something deeper, an earthy scent of old wood, polished stone, and dust, a house suspended in a silence so profound it was almost as if it were holding its breath. Thin shafts of light filtered in through the shutters, illuminating the particles of dust that floated through the air, shimmering like tiny stars in a forgotten galaxy. It felt as though time had slowed here, caught in the folds of the past, and Aanya walked carefully, as if afraid to disturb it.

They moved through the rooms in silence, each step bringing Aanya closer to her grandmother's world. She felt the past in every creak of the floorboards, in every faint scratch on the walls, in the worn edges of the furniture that had once been touched by hands she had never known. Her fingers brushed over everything, the rough grain of the wooden chairs, the delicate lace on the doilies, the faded photographs that hung crooked on the walls. There was a sense of intimacy here, a feeling that every object held a memory, a fragment of Savitri's life hidden in its cracks.

She paused in front of a large wooden wardrobe that stood against the far wall, its doors slightly ajar, revealing a glimpse of fabric within. Aanya hesitated, feeling a strange reverence, and then reached forward, opening the doors fully. Inside, rows of sarees lay neatly folded, their vibrant colours faded to softer hues, emerald greens, deep maroons, and gentle creams, all muted by time but still holding an elegance that seemed to transcend it.

Aanya's fingers trailed over the delicate embroidery of a maroon saree, its golden threads woven in intricate patterns, vines that wound along the borders like whispers of stories kept hidden. She imagined her grandmother draping it over her shoulders, perhaps glancing at herself in a mirror, wondering if someone might one day see her in the way she wanted to be seen, not as someone's daughter or future wife, but simply as herself.

Rohan watched her, his face thoughtful. "Do you think she kept these as a reminder of herself?" he asked gently. "As pieces of her life that no one else could take away?"

Aanya nodded, her voice barely a whisper. "Yes... I think these were the pages of her life that she couldn't share with anyone. They were parts of her dreams, folded away so they wouldn't fade."

They lingered in the house a little longer, Aanya moving slowly through the rooms, her fingers trailing over every surface, every object, until it felt as if she had imprinted herself on the space. Finally, they stepped out into the morning light, and Aanya cast a final, lingering look back, feeling a pang of sadness for the girl her grandmother had once been. She imagined that the house, too, felt a sense of release, as if it had been waiting for her to return, to remember.

Their next destination was the haveli where Dev had lived – a grand, crumbling mansion that stood at the edge of the village, its grandeur softened but not diminished by the years. Even in decay, it held an air of dignity, a quiet elegance that spoke of a time when it had been filled with life and light. Vines climbed its walls, weaving through cracks in the stone, while intricate carvings adorned its arches, faded but still striking, like echoes of laughter lingering in empty rooms.

"This is where he lived," Aanya whispered, her voice barely audible as she took in the vastness of the structure. "Dadi wrote about it so many times, like it was both a wonder and a cage."

Rohan looked around, his gaze lingering on the arches, the broken tiles beneath their feet, and the chandeliers that hung from the ceilings like suspended ghosts. "It's hard to imagine now, but you can almost feel what it must have been like, full of light, music... and yet, he must have felt so alone."

They entered the haveli, their footsteps reverberating through the empty halls. The air was cool, carrying a faint scent of something floral, like dried petals left long ago but whose fragrance had embedded itself into the stone. Dust lay thick on every surface, and the chandeliers caught the light in faint, scattered glimmers, the crystals casting tiny rainbows onto the walls.

As they wandered through the rooms, Aanya's gaze fell on a small alcove hidden behind a heavy velvet curtain, its fabric now a faded, dusty maroon. She pulled the curtain aside and found a stack of letters tied with a delicate, fraying red ribbon. Her heart raced as she untied the ribbon, unfolding the first letter with trembling hands.

The handwriting was elegant, each line carefully penned in Dev's hand. Aanya felt a shiver run through her as she read his words, words that seemed to reach across the years, filling the empty room with the pulse of his love.

"My beloved Savitri, each night is a hollow echo without you. In the world outside, there are walls that keep us apart, but beneath the banyan tree, it is only us. I wish we could find a way beyond these walls, beyond this world that binds us..."

Aanya felt tears pricking at her eyes as she read, each word a testament to a love that had bloomed in secret, hidden but no less real. Dev's love was raw, urgent, filled with a longing that had survived the years on these faded pages.

Rohan leaned over, reading with her, his voice soft. "Their love... it's like something that existed outside of time. Like it only ever really lived in the shadows."

Aanya nodded, her voice catching in her throat. "They were trapped by things they couldn't change. Family, expectations... they were bound by a world that couldn't accept what they felt."

As they moved deeper into the haveli, they found a locked room at the end of a shadowed corridor, the door thick and resistant, as though guarding something precious. Rohan tested the handle, and Aanya's heart pounded as they searched for a key, finally finding one hidden beneath a loose floorboard. With bated breath, she slid it into the lock, feeling the door give way with a low, aching groan.

Inside, the room was dim, the air heavy with the scent of time. A small desk sat against the wall, dust coating its surface, and a diary lay open, its pages brittle and yellowed. Aanya approached it, her fingers trembling as she recognised Dev's handwriting.

"I am leaving Nandipur," the first line read. *"I can't bear to watch her live a life that is not ours. I loved her too much to stay and watch her disappear into a world that could never be mine..."*

A sob caught in Aanya's throat as she read, her heart aching for the man who had loved her grandmother with such intensity that he chose to leave, to carry the weight of their love in silence rather than watch it be taken from them. She imagined him sitting in this room, writing these words, pouring out his heart in a space that had once held their dreams.

Rohan placed a gentle hand on her shoulder, his touch warm and grounding. "He loved her enough to let her go. It was the only gift he could give her."

Aanya closed the diary slowly, her fingers lingering on the worn leather cover as though it held a piece of Dev himself, a fragment of the man who had once lived and loved within these walls. Her breath was shallow, her heart pounding with the intimacy of reading his words and the quiet, aching tenderness that had filled these rooms. For the first time, she could almost see the world as he had seen it—a world that confined and separated him from the woman he loved, yet one he had filled with his own dreams and whispered hopes.

Rohan stood beside her, his gaze watchful, sensing the weight of the moment. "Where to next?" he asked gently, his voice pulling her back to the present.

Aanya glanced around, the vast, dimly lit hallways of the haveli stretching out like pathways into memory. She felt an almost magnetic pull guiding her deeper into the heart of the house. "Let's go through each room," she whispered. "I want to see the spaces he lived in, the places Dadi would have known… maybe even the things they shared, however briefly."

They walked through the grand hallway, their footsteps echoing softly off the stone floors. The air was thick with the scent of aged wood and faint traces of incense that had embedded itself in the walls, like a ghostly reminder of a time when these rooms had been full of life and ritual. Dust lay thick on the surfaces, settling over furniture that had once been polished and admired, each piece a remnant of a life that had moved on while these objects had remained still.

They reached a large, formal sitting room, and Aanya paused, letting her eyes roam over the grand armchairs, the elaborately carved coffee table, and the ornate fireplace that had once served as the centrepiece of family gatherings. The room held an air of stillness, but she could almost see faint traces of its past glory—the distant clinking of teacups, the soft murmur of conversation, the flicker of candlelight casting warm shadows on the walls. She imagined Dev here, his eyes drifting to the door, waiting, hoping for even a fleeting glimpse of her grandmother.

"It must have been lonely for him," Aanya murmured, her voice barely more than a whisper. "Living in all this splendour, but never feeling like it was truly his."

Rohan nodded; his gaze distant as he took in the room. "It's like this place was a cage for him. All this beauty, but he couldn't escape the expectations that came with it."

They moved deeper into the haveli, exploring the rooms one by one. They came upon a study lined with shelves upon shelves of books, their spines faded but still elegant. A layer of dust coated the rows of volumes, yet Aanya felt a sense of warmth emanating from the room, as if it had been a place of solace for Dev. She ran her fingers along the books, their titles nearly obscured by dust and time, but there was an undeniable charm in their weight, their presence.

She pulled one book from the shelf, its leather cover cracked and worn. As she opened it, a single pressed flower fell from between the pages – a delicate marigold, its once-bright petals now a faint, fragile orange. Aanya's heart skipped a beat as she held it in her palm, her mind racing back to Dev's diary, where he had written of a marigold he had tucked into his pocket as a reminder of the day he and Savitri had met.

"Do you think..." Rohan began, his eyes wide as he looked at the faded flower in Aanya's hand.

She nodded, her voice catching. "This was hers, or at least it reminded him of her." She placed it back between the pages with a tenderness that bordered on reverence, closing the book carefully. The small, fragile flower seemed to hold a world of memories, as if the simple act of pressing it between the pages had somehow preserved not just its form, but the emotions woven into it.

They continued, finding small pieces of Dev's life hidden in unexpected places–a tarnished silver bangle, a collection of charcoal sketches tucked into a drawer, each one capturing different facets of the village: the fields in early morning mist, the banyan tree near the temple, a quick sketch of a girl, her face turned away, but her form unmistakable. Aanya's breath caught as she looked at it, recognising the slight tilt of her grandmother's head, the graceful fall of her braid.

"He drew her," she whispered, her voice trembling. "He captured her here, where no one could see, where he could keep her for himself."

Rohan looked over her shoulder, the faintest trace of a smile on his face. "It's like he carried her with him, even when they couldn't be together. This place, it's filled with pieces of her."

They wandered further, moving through a narrow corridor that led to a small, private sitting room. The walls were lined with faded, once-bright tapestries, and a single armchair sat by a window, its upholstery worn but still rich with deep, jewel-toned colours. It was here that Dev had written about finding quiet moments, the rare sanctuary he had from his family's expectations and the village's prying eyes. Aanya could almost feel him there, his thoughts focused on Savitri, a book forgotten in his lap, his gaze drifting out the window towards the distant hills.

She settled into the armchair, running her hand over the armrest. It felt almost intimate, as though she were connecting to him, to his private world. The air was thick with the weight of unspoken words, and for a moment, Aanya felt the overwhelming longing Dev must have carried with him, day after day, as he dreamed of a life that was just beyond his reach.

Rohan watched her with quiet understanding, standing nearby as though giving her space to absorb the room's quiet energy. "He must have sat here, thinking of her," he said softly. "It's like this whole house is a reflection of his love. He hid it away, just like he hid his feelings, but it's still here, waiting for someone to uncover it."

Aanya closed her eyes, letting her mind drift back to the moments described in Dev's letters, the stolen glances and hidden smiles he'd shared with Savitri, the quiet promises exchanged in whispered tones beneath the banyan tree. She could almost feel the weight of his love, so pure and steadfast, yet bound by the limits of the world around him.

After a while, they rose and ventured into the heart of the haveli, following winding corridors and staircases until they reached a secluded balcony. The view stretched out over the village, the rooftops and courtyards spread out below them like a tapestry. Aanya rested her hands on the stone balustrade, feeling the roughness beneath her palms as she looked out, imagining Dev standing here, staring out at the world he yearned to escape, knowing that Savitri was somewhere below, just out of reach.

"This must have been where he dreamed of a life outside these walls," Aanya murmured, her voice filled with both admiration and sadness. "He would have looked out here, feeling like everything he wanted was just beyond his grasp."

Rohan leaned beside her, his gaze distant as he took in the view. "It must have been agony for him, being so close yet so far from her. Every day, carrying that love without being able to share it fully."

They lingered there, the quiet filling the spaces between them, the weight of Dev's love settling over them like a presence. Aanya felt a sense of peace wash over her, a feeling that she had uncovered something sacred that she had seen in a part of her grandmother's life that had remained hidden for so long.

As they made their way back down, they entered a small, dimly lit room off the main hall. A simple writing desk stood in the corner, papers scattered over its surface. Among them, Aanya found a single, folded letter written in Savitri's handwriting. Her heart raced as she recognised the familiar loops and curls of her grandmother's script; the words faded but still clear.

"My dearest Dev, though the world may keep us apart, know that you are in every breath I take, in every sunrise and every dusk. Our love may remain hidden, but it will never be forgotten..."

Aanya's fingers trembled as she read the letter a piece of her grandmother's heart laid bare, a confession written in the shadows yet filled with the strength of her love. She felt tears prick at her eyes, her heart swelling with pride and sorrow for the woman who had been forced to hide so much of herself.

"She loved him with everything she had," Aanya whispered, her voice catching. "Even though they couldn't be together, she never let go of him."

Rohan placed a comforting hand on her shoulder, his eyes filled with understanding. "Their love lives on here, Aanya. It's like these walls, this place... it's kept their story safe all these years, waiting for you to find it."

They stayed in the room a little longer, savouring the quiet intimacy of the space, the whispers of Dev and Savitri's love surrounding them like a soft, unbreakable thread. As they finally made their way out of the haveli, Aanya felt a profound sense of peace, a feeling that she had uncovered the essence of a love that had never truly faded.

Unravelling Truths

As twilight settled over Nandipur, Aanya sat in her small room at the village guesthouse, the quiet enveloping her like a heavy blanket. She had placed Dev's diary and letters in front of her, their worn pages spilling stories that had been locked away in silence. Every word she had read today, every fragment of the love her grandmother had once held in secret, felt like a precious weight in her hands, a piece of herself she had only just begun to discover.

Outside, the faint chirping of crickets mingled with the soft rustle of leaves in the evening breeze, sounds that seemed to echo the aching gentleness of her grandmother's story. Aanya's mind drifted back to the empty rooms of the haveli, the faded sketches, the dried marigold petal pressed in a forgotten book—all the remnants of a love that had endured in silence for decades.

She was pulled from her thoughts by the faint vibration of her phone. Her mother's name appeared on the screen, accompanied by a brief message: *"Aanya, call me as soon as you can. This obsession with Dadi's past... we need to talk."*

Aanya's heart clenched as she read the words, feeling the tension threaded into each one. She knew her mother disapproved of her journey to Nandipur, of her quest to unearth the hidden depths of her grandmother's life. Meera Sharma had always believed in practicality, in looking forward rather than backward. The idea of uncovering forgotten love letters and reliving painful histories was as foreign to her as it was troubling. But Aanya hadn't expected this message, which was so direct and insistent.

She sat there for a moment, the weight of her mother's disapproval pressing down on her, until finally, with a quiet sigh, she dialled the number. The phone barely rang twice before Meera answered, her voice sharp, carrying a tension that crackled through the line like a distant storm.

"Aanya, I don't understand why you're still in Nandipur," Meera began, her tone brisk, laced with irritation. "We've gone through Dadi's things; we've paid our respects. What more are you hoping to find there?"

Aanya took a steadying breath, trying to keep her voice calm. "Mom, I know you don't understand, but there's so much we never knew about Dadi. She had an entire life, a love she never shared with us. I've found letters, sketches, and memories she held onto until the very end. I can't just ignore that. I need to understand her, to know who she really was."

There was a brief pause filled with the distant hum of Meera's silence. When she finally spoke, her voice was edged with frustration. "Aanya, some things are meant to stay in the past. Your Dadi chose to live her life the way she did for a reason. She made her peace. Digging up old memories, especially those that she kept hidden, serves no purpose but to reopen old wounds."

"Mom," Aanya's voice wavered, but she pressed on, determined. "But did she really find peace? Everything I've found here, every word she wrote, every moment she captured... it's clear she carried this love, this ache, with her until the very end. She left parts of herself in these memories, hidden but alive. How can we just ignore that?"

Meera's sigh crackled through the line, a sound filled with years of unresolved emotions. "Aanya, you think you're finding the truth, but there's so much you don't know. Dadi's past isn't just about her and this... Dev. It's about our family, about the choices she made and the consequences we all had to bear. It's about your father, too, and the pain he's carried because of her choices."

Aanya felt a chill settle over her as her mother's words sank in, a ripple of confusion mingling with a deeper sense of unease. "What are you talking about? I thought Dadi was his rock, his guiding light."

Meera's voice softened, yet the bitterness was unmistakable. "Your father loved her, idolised her. As a child, she was everything to him: his role model and his safe place. But when he learned about Dev... it shattered something in him. He couldn't understand why she had kept that part of herself hidden, why she had chosen duty over the man she loved. He felt betrayed by Aanya. Betrayed by a woman he thought he knew completely."

Aanya sat in stunned silence, her mind racing. The idea of her father, a man who had always seemed steady and reserved, carrying his own private wound because of her grandmother's secret love felt like a truth too heavy to bear. "But... but why didn't she tell him? Or any of us?"

"Because she believed that some things were better left unsaid," Meera replied, her voice thick with a weariness Aanya had rarely heard. "She wanted a peaceful life for her family, a life free from the burdens of the past. But that doesn't mean your father didn't feel hurt, that he didn't carry the weight of her choices. To him, Dadi was a symbol of honour and sacrifice, someone who embodied the values of family and duty. Learning about Dev... it made him feel like she had chosen something else, someone else, over him."

Aanya's voice trembled as she struggled to reconcile this new layer of her family's history. "But... didn't he understand that she must have had her reasons? That she was young, that love isn't always simple?"

Meera's voice was barely more than a whisper, as though dredging up memories she'd kept buried for too long. "Maybe he understood, but understanding doesn't always bring forgiveness. It was a betrayal, Aanya, a betrayal he never really healed from. And seeing you chase after Dadi's past… it brings all of that back for him. He sees it as you choosing her hidden life, her hidden love, over the life she built with us."

The weight of her mother's words settled heavily over Aanya, a realisation that left her breathless. She had been so focused on uncovering her grandmother's story, on piecing together the fragments of a love that had remained hidden, that she hadn't considered how it might affect those who had lived in the shadow of that story.

"Mom," she began, her voice quiet, almost pleading. "I didn't mean to hurt him or you. I just… I feel like Dadi's story is a part of me, too. I can't just pretend it doesn't matter."

"Aanya," Meera's voice softened, but there was still an edge to her tone, a finality that seemed to carry the weight of generations. "You're unearthing things that were buried for a reason. Your Dadi chose to keep this love hidden, to let it rest. Please, think about what this is doing to our family. Think about your father."

"I have, Mom," Aanya replied, a new determination settling over her. "I have thought about all of it. But Dadi's choices shaped all of us, even if we didn't know it. And ignoring her story, pretending it never existed… that feels like erasing a part of her and a part of myself."

The silence that followed was heavy, filled with words that neither mother nor daughter could speak aloud. Finally, Meera's voice came through, quieter now, a hint of resignation colouring her words. "If you truly believe that, Aanya, then I won't stop you. But just know that you're opening doors that were closed for a reason. You're bringing back wounds that never fully healed."

Aanya closed her eyes, feeling the tension radiate through her, a mixture of guilt and defiance. "I understand, Mom. I promise I'll be careful. I won't let this tear us apart. But I need to do this. For Dadi. And for myself."

After a quiet goodbye, Aanya hung up, her phone still warm in her hand as she stared at the letters and diary spread out before her. Her mother's words echoed in her mind, a reminder of the complex, tangled web of love, duty, resentment, and sacrifice that had shaped her family's history. The revelation that her father had carried a private pain, a betrayal that had quietly altered the course of their family, added weight to her journey that she hadn't anticipated.

For a long while, she sat in silence, letting the threads of her family's past intertwine with her own thoughts. Her heart ached for her father, for the boy who had adored his mother only to have his idealised image of her shattered. She felt a pang of sorrow for her mother, too, who had watched this silent wound fester, unable to bridge the gap between the woman her husband had loved and the reality of her hidden life.

But most of all, Aanya's heart ached for herself, for the girl she had been, for the woman she was becoming, for the weight of her family's secrets that had shaped her without her even knowing. She was no longer just a granddaughter seeking to understand her Dadi's love story; she was now a link in a chain, carrying the burden of her family's past, each revelation a stitch in a tapestry woven from love, loss, and longing.

As she sat there, the crickets outside faded into silence, replaced by the quiet hum of the night settling over the village. She felt the weight of her journey pressing down on her, but within that weight, she also felt a quiet resolve. She knew now that this path would not be easy, that it would demand both love and strength to carry forward. But it was a journey she needed to continue, not just for herself, but for the women who had come before her, for the love stories that had shaped her family, both spoken and unspoken.

At that moment, Aanya realised that her journey was no longer just about uncovering her grandmother's past. It was about embracing the complex, imperfect legacy she had inherited, a legacy shaped by choices, by heartbreak, and by the enduring strength of women who had loved deeply, even when the world wouldn't let them speak of it.

Reflections of the Heart

The late afternoon sun cast a warm, honeyed light over Nandipur, filtering through the dense canopy of trees that arched over the quiet village paths. Aanya and Rohan walked in companionable silence; their footsteps slow, almost hesitant, as if they, too, were caught in the stillness that blanketed the village. Each step felt heavy, resonant with the stories they had uncovered, the memories and emotions that had seeped into the very earth around them.

Aanya clutched her grandmother's letters close to her chest, her fingers brushing over the fragile, yellowed paper as if she could feel her grandmother's heartbeat in words. She had spent days uncovering Dev and Savitri's love story—a love that had grown in stolen moments, in quiet spaces, a love that had thrived despite the limitations forced upon it. And as much as she felt connected to their story, as much as she admired the depth of their devotion, she found herself increasingly torn, grappling with a feeling that had begun to stir deep within her heart.

She felt the warmth of Rohan beside her, his steady presence like a balm against her tangled thoughts. They reached a quiet spot by the riverbank, where the water moved gently, catching the last of the sunlight in golden ripples. The air was filled with the earthy scent of damp soil, mingling with the faint sweetness of wild jasmine that grew along the river's edge. It was the kind of place that invited secrets, the kind of place where silence felt sacred.

Without a word, Aanya sat down on a moss-covered stone, her gaze drifting over the river as she pulled one of Dev's letters from the stack. She unfolded the paper carefully, feeling the delicate crinkle beneath her fingertips, as if each crease, each faded line, held a memory, a whisper from the past. She glanced at Rohan, who had settled beside her, his expression thoughtful, his eyes filled with a quiet curiosity that seemed to mirror her own.

Taking a deep breath, she began to read aloud, her voice soft, reverent, as if calling Dev's spirit into the present.

"Savitri,

I never planned to love you. I thought we were only friends, two people bound by laughter and shared stories. But there are moments when I see you, really see you, and it undoes me. Your smile is the light I seek in every dark corner, your laughter the music that fills my silence. And though I may never say it aloud, I love you as surely as the river finds its way to the sea."

Aanya's voice trembled as she finished, the words hanging in the air like a prayer, delicate and profound. She felt the ache of Dev's unspoken love, the quiet yearning that filled each line. She could almost see him, standing beside Savitri beneath the shade of an old banyan tree, his heart in his eyes, too afraid to say the words out loud.

She glanced at Rohan, her heart pounding as she saw the understanding in his gaze. "They started as friends," she murmured, almost to herself. "They didn't mean to fall in love. It just... happened. And when they finally realised it, it was already too late to turn back."

Rohan's eyes softened, his gaze steady as he looked at her. "Love has a way of finding us when we least expect it. Sometimes, it begins in friendship, in the smallest gestures, the quietest moments. And then one day, you realise that it's become something more, something you can't ignore."

Aanya felt a flutter in her chest, a warmth that spread through her like sunlight breaking through clouds. She thought back to her own memories with Rohan–the years of friendship, the laughter, the silent comfort he had offered her on countless occasions. She thought of the way he had listened without judgement, the way he had stood by her side through everything, his presence steady, grounding as if he had always been meant to be there.

She opened another letter, her fingers lingering over the worn edges as she read Dev's words, her voice barely a whisper.

"There are days when I tell myself that friendship is enough, that I am strong enough to bear this love alone. But when I am with you, Savitri, my heart betrays me. I think of the future, of all the moments we may never share, and it is an ache I carry in silence. How cruel it is to love with such certainty and yet know that we will always remain apart. But if friendship is all we are given, then I will love you quietly, in the spaces between our words."

Aanya felt her throat tighten, her chest swelling with an emotion she couldn't quite name. She looked at Rohan, her cheeks warm, her heart racing as she saw the gentle intensity in his eyes. Dev's words felt like a mirror, reflecting feelings she hadn't dared to acknowledge until now, a quiet, unspoken love that had been growing between them, nurtured in friendship and patience.

She tried to speak, but the words caught in her throat, tangled with the realisation that had begun to dawn upon her. Rohan seemed to sense her hesitation, his gaze steady, unhurried, as if giving her the time she needed to find her way.

"Dev loved her in silence," Aanya said finally, her voice soft, barely more than a whisper. "He loved her in the spaces between their words, in the quiet moments when they were just... together. I wonder if that's how love grows. In those unspoken places, in the moments we don't even realise we're sharing."

Rohan nodded, his voice gentle. "Sometimes, love doesn't need words, Aanya. It lives in the smallest gestures, in the quiet of just being with someone. Maybe that's what Dev and Savitri had. A love that didn't need to be declared; it just existed, quietly, waiting."

Aanya felt a tremor run through her, a quiet thrill mingling with a strange, bittersweet ache. She thought back to the countless moments she had shared with Rohan, the way his hand had steadied her as they climbed the narrow steps of the haveli, the way he had been there in the silence, his presence a balm she hadn't even realised she needed. Each memory felt like a gentle nudge, a reminder of something she had been too afraid to see.

Her fingers brushed over the edge of another letter, one that seemed hastily written; the ink smudged in places as if Dev had poured his heart onto the page in a moment of desperate clarity.

"Savitri, there are things I will never say aloud, but I hope you feel them in my presence. Every time we meet, I feel as though my heart is laid bare, as though you see

into the deepest part of me. If friendship is all we are given, then I will love you in the spaces, in the silences that speak louder than anything I could ever say. My love will live in the unspoken."

Aanya felt her heart beat faster, her pulse quickening as she read, her hands trembling slightly as she closed the letter. She looked at Rohan, her voice filled with vulnerability she could no longer hide. "Dev loved her... so deeply, so completely. Even when he couldn't say it, he let his love live in the silence, in the spaces where words failed."

Rohan's gaze held hers, his eyes warm and steady. "Maybe that's how it was meant to be for them, a love that could only exist in the quiet, hidden away from the world. But that doesn't mean our love stories have to follow the same path, Aanya."

Aanya felt her cheeks flush, her heart swelling with a realisation that left her both exhilarated and terrified. She had been so absorbed in her grandmother's story, so captivated by the intensity of Dev and Savitri's love, that she hadn't allowed herself to see the quiet love that had been growing right beside her.

They sat in silence, the river's gentle murmur filling the space between them, the sunlight casting a soft glow over the world around them. Aanya glanced down at the letters, at the words that had brought her grandmother's hidden love to life, and felt a quiet resolve settle within her. She didn't need to mirror Dev and Savitri's story, and she didn't need to live a love bound by secrecy or yearning. Her love—if she dared to let herself feel it—could be something softer, something that grew from the simplicity of friendship, from the gentle moments shared in silence.

She closed her eyes, letting herself sink into the warmth of the moment, the warmth of Rohan's presence beside her. She felt his hand reach out, his fingers brushing against hers, a quiet touch that spoke volumes. They didn't need to speak, didn't need to say the words that lingered on the tip of her tongue. She knew, at that moment, that whatever they had, whatever was growing between them, would be nurtured in its own time, allowed to breathe and exist without the weight of unspoken expectations.

They stayed there until the sun began to dip below the horizon, casting the river in shades of amber and rose. Aanya watched the fading light, feeling a quiet peace settle over her, a sense of belonging she hadn't felt in a long time. She glanced at Rohan, her heart swelling with gratitude, with a love she was finally ready to accept, even if she wasn't ready to say it aloud.

As they walked back to the village, side by side, their hands brushing but never quite touching, Aanya felt a profound sense of connection, not just to her grandmother, but to herself, to the love that had been waiting patiently, silently, for her to recognise it. She knew as they walked through the fading light, that her story would be different from Dev and Savitri's. But in its own way, it would be just as real, just as powerful.

And as the shadows lengthened, casting the village in a soft twilight, Aanya felt her heart settle, felt the quiet truth of her love for Rohan bloom within her, waiting for the day she would finally be ready to bring it into the light.

Unseen Bonds

The following morning dawned with a hushed beauty over Nandipur, the early light filtering gently through Aanya's window, filling her room with a warm, golden glow. She had spent the night with her grandmother's letters and Dev's words, absorbing each one as if they were pieces of her own heart. But as much as she felt connected to Savitri's hidden love, Aanya sensed there was a part of her grandmother's story she hadn't yet uncovered, a chapter she needed to understand.

After a quiet breakfast, she made her way to Chandrika's house. The woman who had been Savitri's childhood friend, her confidante, the keeper of so many secrets that had been lost to time. Chandrika's home was a modest one, set back from the village's main path, surrounded by flowering vines and shaded by an ancient neem tree. The air was thick with the scent of marigold, and Aanya felt a familiar warmth as she entered, a sense that she was walking into a place that had known and loved her family.

Chandrika greeted her with a knowing smile, her eyes glinting with the wisdom of age and experience. "I knew you'd be back," she said, her voice filled with warmth. "You look like you have questions, child."

Aanya nodded, feeling the weight of those unasked questions settle over her. "I do, Aunty. I feel like I'm beginning to understand Dadi's story with Dev. But I can't help but wonder... what about her husband, my grandfather? How did he fit into all of this? Was he a part of Dadi's sorrow, or... did he love her in his own way?"

Chandrika's expression softened, her gaze drifting out of the window as if searching for something just beyond reach. "Rajesh Sharma was a good man," she began, her voice touched with a sadness that seemed to echo through the years. "Your grandfather loved Savitri, truly and deeply, but he was trapped, just like she was. Trapped in a life that had been arranged for him, bound by family expectations, by rules he could never bring himself to break."

Aanya felt a pang in her chest as she listened, her heart aching for a man she had only ever known through faded memories and brief family stories. She looked back at Chandrika, a question forming on her lips. "Did he know? About Dev, I mean? About Dadi's love for him?"

Chandrika nodded slowly, her gaze turning thoughtful. "He knew, though Savitri never spoke of it directly. But he was a perceptive man. He saw the shadow in her eyes, the longing she tried to hide. He felt it in the silences between them, in the way she would look away, as though her heart belonged to someone beyond his reach."

Aanya swallowed, her voice thick with emotion. "How did he live with it? Knowing he could never have all of her?"

Chandrika sighed, her fingers tracing an idle pattern on the table as if seeking comfort in the familiar touch of worn wood. "Your grandfather was a man of steadfast resilience." He loved her deeply, Aanya, even though he knew her heart had been touched by another. He once told me that he saw love as a kind of service, a devotion that didn't demand anything in return. He believed that just by caring for her, by giving her a life of peace and stability, he could make her happy."

Aanya closed her eyes, imagining the man her grandfather must have been, a man who had accepted his wife's unspoken love for another, who had chosen to love her without expecting her heart in return. It was a kind of love she hadn't encountered before, a love that didn't demand reciprocation or validation, a love that existed simply for the sake of giving.

"But... did Dadi love him back?" she asked softly, her voice barely more than a whisper.

Chandrika looked at her with a gentle, knowing expression. "Yes, Aanya. She loved him in her own way. Not with the same fire, the same passion she had for Dev. But she respected Rajesh, admired him, and even grew fond of him over the years. He became her friend, her partner in life, even if he was never her first love."

Aanya felt her throat tighten, her heart aching for her grandmother, who had been caught between love and duty, between a man who had claimed her heart and a man who had given her his. She looked down at her hands, the weight of her grandmother's choices pressing upon her.

"Rajesh never resented her, you know," Chandrika continued, her voice soft and reflective. "He understood the complexities of her heart. In his own way, he was grateful for her presence, even if he could never fully claim her love. He once told me that some loves are quiet, that they don't need to be seen to be real."

Aanya's mind drifted back to the letters, to the love her grandmother had hidden, and she realised that her grandfather had also carried his own quiet love, one that he had kept as a silent companion through the years. She wondered how it must have felt for him to live a life devoted to a woman who could only offer him fragments of her heart.

Chandrika leaned back, her gaze thoughtful. "There was a time, in the early years of their marriage, when Savitri felt guilty, burdened by the love she couldn't give Rajesh. But he reassured her, told her that he understood, that he didn't expect her to change. And slowly, that understanding became the foundation of their life together. They found peace in each other's presence, in the companionship they shared. It may not have been the love she had dreamed of, but it was a love they created together."

Aanya felt tears pricking her eyes, her heart aching with a newfound respect for her grandfather, a man who had loved with a kind of grace she hadn't known was possible. She thought back to her parents and her mother's hesitations about her journey and wondered if this knowledge, this acceptance, had been passed down through the generations, a quiet resilience, a love that didn't need words.

She looked up at Chandrika, her voice choked with emotion. "He loved her, didn't he? Even if he knew he could never be her great love, he loved her all the same."

Chandrika nodded, her eyes misty with her own memories. "Yes, child. Rajesh Sharma loved her as a friend, a partner, and a companion. And in the end, that love was just as real as any other."

Aanya rose to leave for lunch, her heart swelling with deep gratitude for the man her grandfather had been –

a man who had loved without expecting, who had given without asking for anything in return. As she walked back through the village, she felt a new understanding, a respect for the complexities of her family's history. It was a legacy of quiet, resilient love, a love that had endured in silence yet had shaped each generation that followed.

And in that moment, Aanya knew that her family's story was more than just one of passion and hidden romance. It was a story of love in all its forms, of friendships that grew into companionship, of loves that could never be spoken, of bonds that transcended the boundaries of expectation. And she, too, was a part of that story, carrying forward a legacy of strength, of quiet resilience, of love that lived in the spaces between.

Shadows of Opposition

A anya returned to Chandrika's house later that afternoon, her heart heavy with the weight of her grandmother's story. Each new revelation felt like peeling back layers of Savitri's life, uncovering the hidden struggles, the loves, and losses that had shaped her. But as much as Aanya had learned, she sensed there was still more, a deeper reason why Savitri's love for Dev had remained hidden and unspoken. And Chandrika, with her wealth of memories, seemed to hold the answers.

As Aanya stepped into Chandrika's home, she noticed the older woman was seated by the small wooden chest that held her precious keepsakes, her fingers carefully sifting through a bundle of letters and trinkets. Chandrika looked up with a soft, almost sorrowful smile as Aanya approached.

"There is something I think you should see, beta," Chandrika said, her voice touched with a sadness that seemed to transcend the years. She pulled out an old, worn envelope, the edges yellowed with time, the ink smudged but still legible. Aanya's heart skipped a beat as she saw the name written in an unfamiliar, formal hand–*Ammaji,* her great-grandmother.

Chandrika handed her the letter, her gaze lingering on it as though it held a world of memories. "This letter was written by Dhaniram Malhotra, Dev's father. It was addressed to your great-grandmother, Savitri's mother. I remember the day it arrived as if it were only yesterday. The village was hushed, and there was an air of tension everywhere. No one said a word, but we all felt it."

Aanya took a steadying breath as she unfolded the fragile paper, her fingers trembling slightly as she read the bold, unyielding words.

"To Ammaji,

I write this with the utmost respect and a heavy heart. Our families, while respectful of one another, belong to different social standings and castes. It would be unwise— and dangerous—for us to consider uniting in such a way. I understand that our children, Dev and Savitri, may have developed an affection, but this is not a union that can bring honour to either family. It is best that you advise Savitri to keep her distance from my son, as I have done the same with him. Any further pursuit of this relationship would

bring shame to both households, and I cannot permit my
son to defy these boundaries. I trust you will see the wisdom
in this and make the appropriate decision.

Respectfully,

Dhaniram Malhotra"

Aanya's heart tightened with each line, her chest aching as she imagined the impact these words must have had on her grandmother. The letter was cold and formal, yet beneath its stiff language lay a threat, a reminder of the unforgiving boundaries drawn by society. Her fingers traced the faded ink, the harshness of each word echoing in her mind, filling her with a quiet rage.

Chandrika watched her with a knowing gaze, her eyes filled with both sympathy and sorrow. "When Ammaji received this letter, she didn't take long to make her decision," Chandrika said, her voice thick with the weight of her memories. "She summoned Savitri, and I watched from outside as they had one of the hardest conversations I'd ever witnessed. I knew, from the look on Savitri's face, that she had already guessed the letter's contents. But hearing it aloud from her own mother... it shattered something in her."

Aanya looked up, her eyes stinging with unshed tears. "What happened after that, Aunty? How did Dadi respond?"

Chandrika took a deep breath, her voice soft and trembling. "Savitri was silent. She didn't fight, didn't argue. She was always a dutiful daughter, always mindful of her family's expectations. But there was a defiance in her eyes, a quiet strength that told me she wasn't ready to give up, even if she couldn't speak it aloud."

She paused, her gaze drifting to the window as though seeing the past play out before her. "After that, Ammaji called upon her brothers, Savitri's uncles. They came from nearby villages, and they were determined to keep the family's honour intact, no matter what. They confronted Savitri and threatened her, saying that if she didn't put an end to this 'nonsense,' they would see to it that she'd be sent away somewhere where she'd never see Dev again."

Aanya felt a chill run through her, a visceral reaction to the image of her grandmother being cornered and coerced, her love treated as a shameful secret to be buried. "They threatened to send her away?"

Chandrika nodded, her voice thick with emotion. "Yes. They told her that she was risking everything: the family's reputation and their standing in the village. They didn't understand her love; to them, it was an insult, a disgrace. And they would not allow it."

Aanya clenched her fists, anger simmering within her at the thought of her grandmother being forced to make such a choice, being torn away from the man she loved.

She looked at Chandrika, her voice tight with sorrow and frustration. "Did Dadi ever speak about it? About how it felt to be given such an ultimatum?"

Chandrika's eyes filled with sadness, her hand reaching out to gently pat Aanya's arm. "Savitri spoke to me, but only once, the night after her family confronted her. She came to my home, her face pale, her hands trembling. I could see that the fire within her had been dimmed, that she had resigned herself to the reality of her situation. She told me that her heart was breaking, that she felt as though she was being torn apart."

Aanya closed her eyes, her mind conjuring the image of her grandmother, young and full of dreams, being forced to watch them crumble, powerless to change her fate. She could almost feel the weight of that heartache, the grief of knowing that the love she held so dear could never be. "How did she survive it, Aunty? How did she move forward?"

Chandrika's gaze softened, her voice a mixture of admiration and sorrow. "Savitri was stronger than any of us. She chose to survive by burying her love deep within her heart, hiding it away where no one could reach it. She poured herself into her family, into her duties, hoping that it would lessen the ache. And when Rajesh came into her life, she did her best to be a good wife to him. She learned to find peace in the life she was given, even if a part of her was left behind."

Aanya felt tears slipping down her cheeks, her chest tightening as she thought of the sacrifices her grandmother had made, the love she had hidden away, bound by societal chains. "Do you think... do you think she ever regretted it? Not fighting back?"

Chandrika's expression grew thoughtful, a bittersweet smile touching her lips. "She did, in her own way. But Savitri found a kind of strength in her choice, Aanya. She made peace with her decision, even if it hurt. And over time, she found solace in her life with Rajesh, in the family they built together. She didn't erase Dev from her heart, but she found a way to live, to give her love where she could."

Aanya looked down at the letter again, feeling the sharp contrast between the warmth of her grandmother's love for Dev and the cold, unyielding language of Dhaniram's words. The letter had torn her grandmother's world apart, yet she had endured and had chosen a life of quiet strength rather than a love that would have brought chaos and rejection.

Chandrika's voice broke into her thoughts. "Dev knew, of course, that his family's approval was never going to be given. He wanted to fight, to take her away, but he respected her choice. When he saw how deeply her family's honour mattered to her, he stepped back. It was his final gift to her, to let her go."

Aanya's heart ached with profound sorrow as she imagined Dev watching the love of his life slip through his fingers, his love left to echo in silence, unspoken but unforgotten. She understood now, more than ever, the sacrifices her grandmother had made and the quiet strength she had carried with her through the years.

She looked at Chandrika, her voice barely more than a whisper. "Thank you, Aunty. Thank you for sharing this with me."

Chandrika gave her a gentle smile, her eyes shining with tears of her own. "Savitri wanted you to know, Aanya. I believe that's why she left the diary, why she left the letters. She wanted someone to carry her story forward, someone who would understand the strength it took to love so deeply, yet to let it go."

Aanya folded the letter carefully, placing it back into the worn envelope. She felt a deep gratitude, not only for the story she now carried but for the resilience her grandmother had passed down, the quiet strength that lived within her. As she left Chandrika's home, the weight of her family's history settled over her like a mantle, a reminder of the legacy of love, loss, and endurance that she now carried forward.

And with every step, she felt her grandmother's spirit beside her, guiding her, a whisper of courage echoing through the generations. Aanya knew that while she couldn't change the past, she could honour it, embrace it, and live her life with the strength and love Savitri had taught her, a love that was quiet but unbreakable, a love that had survived in the shadows.

Echoes of the Past

⬥⬥⬥

The days in Nandipur had grown heavy with the weight of revelation after revelation, each piece of her grandmother's past weaving together a story that was as haunting as it was beautiful. Aanya had thought she was prepared for the secrets hidden within her family's history, but each discovery seemed to lead her deeper, binding her to a love that had been silenced yet never fully lost.

That morning, she and Rohan decided to explore the quieter edges of Nandipur, hoping the fresh air and open fields might offer a reprieve from the intensity of the recent days. They walked along the narrow path that wound through the village, leading them to a secluded grove just outside Nandipur's borders. The trees cast long shadows over the ground, the air filled with the earthy scent of the countryside, punctuated by the occasional call of a distant bird. Amidst the serenity, Aanya felt her grandmother's presence, not as an urging to uncover more but as a quiet reassurance that what she had found was enough to carry forward.

As they walked, a figure appeared up ahead, standing near a small shrine that looked as though it had been untouched for years. The man, tall and lean with a shock of white hair, had an air of authority, even in his relaxed stance. He wore a simple kurta, but there was a presence about him that made Aanya's breath hitch. Rohan noticed her pause, his gaze following hers until he, too, spotted the man.

The man turned as they approached, his sharp eyes assessing them with a look that held both curiosity and caution. He gave them a polite nod, his gaze lingering on Aanya as though he saw something familiar in her face.

"Namaste," he greeted his voice deep, carrying the remnants of a once-commanding tone softened by age. "You must be the young woman I've heard about, the one asking questions about Dev Malhotra and Savitri Sharma."

Aanya's heart leapt at the mention of their names. She exchanged a quick glance with Rohan, who gave her a slight nod of encouragement before she turned back to the man.

"Yes, I am," she replied, her voice steady despite the flutter in her chest. "I'm Aanya Sharma, Savitri's granddaughter. And... forgive me, but who are you?"

The man's gaze softened, a faint smile touching his lips. "Ah, of course. My name is Vijay Deshmukh. I was an inspector here in Nandipur many years ago. I knew Dev, as well as your grandmother. I remember them both well."

Aanya's pulse quickened, the weight of his words settling over her. This man, this retired inspector, held memories of the two people who had shaped her journey, who had loved each other in the quiet, forbidden spaces of their lives.

"Inspector Deshmukh," she said slowly, feeling a spark of hope. "I've been trying to understand what happened to them, to learn more about my grandmother's life and the love she carried. But there are so many gaps, so many things that were never spoken of. If you know anything, please share it with us."

Deshmukh's face grew sombre, his expression touched with a sadness that seemed to transcend time. He gestured towards a nearby bench beneath the shade of an old banyan tree, its twisted roots digging deep into the earth. They settled onto the bench, the inspector folding his hands as he looked out at the distant hills, his gaze distant and reflective.

"What I am about to tell you, Aanya," he began, his voice quiet and steady, "is something I haven't shared with anyone in a very long time. But perhaps it's time for the truth to see the light now that you're here, searching for answers."

He took a deep breath, and Aanya felt Rohan's hand brush against hers, a silent reassurance. She braced herself, sensing that whatever Deshmukh was about to reveal would alter everything she thought she knew.

"Dev Malhotra was a good man," Deshmukh started, his tone heavy with emotion. "He was quiet and thoughtful, but there was a fire in him, a desire to break free from the rules that bound him. He loved your grandmother with every fibre of his being. I think he would have gone to the ends of the earth for her if he could. But circumstances were against them from the start."

Aanya nodded, her heart aching with each word, already familiar with the tragic constraints that had torn them apart. "I know they couldn't be together. I know about the opposition from their families, from society..."

Deshmukh gave a sad smile. "Yes, their love was not meant to be, at least not in the eyes of those who held power. But Dev wasn't one to give up easily. He tried, again and again, to find a way for them to be together. There were rumours in the village, whispers that he had plans to leave, to escape with her and start a life far from here."

Aanya's eyes widened, her heart beating faster. "Did Dadi... did she know?"

Deshmukh nodded. "Yes. She knew. I believe they were on the verge of running away, of taking a risk despite the consequences. But then something happened, something that changed everything."

He paused, his gaze darkening as he leaned forward, his voice dropping to a near whisper. "One night, Dev went missing. There were reports that he had been seen arguing with his father, Dhaniram, just before he vanished. The next morning, I was called to investigate, but by then, it was as if he had disappeared into thin air. We searched for days, but there was no trace of him, no sign of where he had gone."

Aanya's breath caught, a cold dread creeping over her as Deshmukh's words settled in. "You mean… he just vanished? No one saw him after that?"

The inspector's face grew even graver, his eyes filled with an old, unhealed sorrow. "Yes, Aanya. No one ever saw him again. And without a body, without any evidence, his father insisted that he had simply left, gone to start a new life. But many of us… we suspected otherwise."

Aanya's hands trembled, the implications of his words sinking in. "You think… you think he was killed, don't you?"

Deshmukh hesitated, his voice barely more than a whisper. "We had our suspicions. There were whispers and rumours that Dev had paid the price for defying his family, for daring to dream of a life that broke the boundaries of caste and tradition. But without proof, I could do nothing. And over time, the village let it fade into silence, a tragedy no one spoke of."

Aanya felt a crushing sorrow settle over her, a grief that seemed to echo through the years. Dev, the man her grandmother had loved, had disappeared without a trace, his life cut short simply because he had dared to love across boundaries drawn by others.

"Dadi... did she know?" she asked, her voice choked with emotion.

Deshmukh looked away, his gaze distant, haunted. "She knew, Aanya. She felt it, I believe, in her heart. She waited, hoping that perhaps one day he would come back. But as the years passed, she came to accept the truth. Dev wasn't coming back, and she had to move on. She buried her love, her sorrow, and lived the life her family had chosen for her."

Aanya's vision blurred with tears, her heart breaking for her grandmother, for the love that had been stolen from her, a love that had never been allowed to flourish. Rohan's hand tightened around hers, his presence grounding her, offering comfort amidst the pain.

"So... all these years, Dadi carried this grief, this unanswered question, never knowing for certain what happened to him," she whispered, her voice filled with sorrow.

Deshmukh nodded, his own eyes misty. "Yes, and it changed her. She became quieter, more reserved. She poured herself into her family and into her duties, but there was always a part of her that remained with him, that longed for the life they might have had. And now, Aanya, you've come here, stirring up these old memories, bringing back the love they shared."

Aanya wiped her eyes, her heart swelling with a fierce determination. She looked at Deshmukh, her voice steady despite the tremor within. "Thank you for telling me, Inspector. I needed to know. Dadi deserved someone to remember, someone to carry forward the truth."

Deshmukh gave a slow nod, his expression both weary and relieved. "I hope that sharing this will help you find peace, Aanya. I hope that by remembering, you'll give their story the ending they never had."

As they parted ways, Aanya felt the weight of her grandmother's story settle more heavily upon her. This journey had begun as a quest for understanding, a way to connect with a woman she had loved but never truly known. Now, it had become something far greater. She was no longer just uncovering a story; she was giving voice to a love that had been silenced, to a life that had been cut short. And she knew, with a clarity she hadn't felt before, that she wouldn't rest until she had uncovered every piece of it and her grandmother's love had been given the remembrance it deserved.

Rohan walked beside her, his hand still clasped in hers, his presence a steady, comforting force. As they walked back to the village, the sun dipping lower on the horizon, Aanya felt a renewed sense of purpose, a quiet resolve to carry her grandmother's story forward, to honour the love she had been forced to bury, and to find peace in the truth, no matter how painful.

In that moment, she felt her grandmother's spirit beside her, a presence woven from love and resilience, urging her forward, guiding her through the shadows of the past towards a brighter, more hopeful future.

Shadows of Betrayal

The evening shadows stretched long over Nandipur, casting a melancholic glow that seemed to echo Aanya's own heart. She sat across from Chandrika, the older woman's face illuminated by the soft light of a single lantern. Chandrika's gaze was distant, her eyes filled with memories too painful to share easily. But Aanya sensed that tonight, she would finally uncover the part of her grandmother's story that had remained hidden, even from her deepest imaginings.

Chandrika clasped Aanya's hands tightly, her fingers cold yet steady. She took a deep breath, and Aanya could feel the tension in her grip as if she were holding back a lifetime of secrets.

"There is something I've kept from you, child," Chandrika began, her voice heavy, almost reluctant. "Something about your grandmother... and your family's role in her tragedy."

Aanya's heart clenched, the weight of the moment settling over her. She had spent days piecing together the love story of Dev and Savitri, but she had never suspected that her family—the people who should have protected and cherished her grandmother—had played a part in tearing their love apart.

"Please, Aunty," she whispered, her voice trembling. "Tell me everything. I need to know."

Chandrika closed her eyes as if gathering strength and began to speak, her voice thick with sorrow. "Your grandmother and Dev... they didn't just face opposition from the village or from society, Aanya. It was much closer. Her own family... couldn't bear the idea of her love for a man outside their caste. And the one who led that opposition, the one who hurt her most deeply, was her own brother: Neeraj."

Aanya's breath hitched, a wave of disbelief washing over her. "Neeraj? Dadi's brother? But... I've heard so many stories about him, how he was her protector, her closest confidant. How could he–"

Chandrika interrupted gently, her gaze filled with regret. "Neeraj loved his sister, yes. But he loved the family's honour more. When he found out about Dev, he felt it was his duty to put a stop to it, to bring her back to what he saw as her 'senses.' In his mind, her love was a disgrace, a stain on their family's name. He thought he was protecting her, even if his way of doing so destroyed her."

Aanya's hands trembled, her fingers clenching around Chandrika's. "But... how could he do that to her, Aunty? How could he betray her like that?"

Chandrika's face softened; her eyes filled with a sorrow that seemed to transcend the years. "Because he was blinded by pride, by the rigid rules he had been raised to uphold. He believed he was saving her from shame, from a life he thought would only bring her pain. But what he didn't see was that his actions were the true cause of her suffering."

Aanya shook her head, her mind reeling with the enormity of it all. "What... what did he do? How far did he go to stop her?"

Chandrika looked away, her gaze distant as she relived the painful memories. "When Neeraj found out about her love for Dev, he confronted her and forced her to choose between her family and her heart. I remember that day as if it were yesterday. Savitri came to me afterwards, her face pale, her eyes red from crying. She told me that Neeraj had threatened to cut her off, to send her away if she didn't break things off with Dev."

Aanya's heart shattered at the image of her grandmother standing before her own brother, pleading for the chance to live the life she wanted, only to be met with threats and ultimatums. She could almost see her, her gentle, quiet Dadi, torn between the loyalty she felt for her family and the love that had become her very breath.

"She must have been devastated," Aanya whispered, her voice thick with emotion. "How could she go on, knowing her own brother—her own family—saw her love as a crime?"

Chandrika nodded, her voice trembling. "She was child. But that wasn't the worst of it. Neeraj didn't stop there. When he saw that his threats hadn't broken her, that she was still seeing Dev, he went further. He... he went to Dev's family. He told them everything, painted their love as something shameful, something that would ruin both families."

Aanya's stomach twisted, her heart breaking as she realised the full extent of her uncle's betrayal. Her own family—her blood—had not only forbidden her grandmother's love but had gone so far as to ensure Dev's family would oppose it and that no corner of their lives would be untouched by judgement and scorn.

"What did Dadi do when she found out?" she asked, her voice barely more than a whisper.

Chandrika's eyes filled with tears as she recalled the look in Savitri's eyes that day. "She came to me, broken. She didn't speak for the longest time, just sat there, staring into the distance. I could see that something inside her had died. When she finally spoke, she said, 'They have taken my love, Chandrika. They have turned it into something ugly, something I must hide.' She didn't even cry, Aanya. She just sat there like a ghost."

Aanya's own tears spilt over, her chest aching with the image of her grandmother, forced to hide the one thing that had given her life meaning, the love that had been her light in a world that demanded obedience. "She... she must have felt so alone," she murmured, her voice choked with grief.

"She did, child," Chandrika replied, her voice thick with her own tears. "She was alone, surrounded by people who saw her love as a stain on their honour, who didn't care that they were tearing her apart. And Neeraj... he took it upon himself to ensure that she would never be with Dev. He threatened to tell the whole village, to shame her publicly if she ever dared defy him."

Aanya felt a surge of anger, a fierce protectiveness rising within her for the grandmother who had been forced to carry this burden, this betrayal, in silence. "How could he do that to her, Aunty? How could he claim to love her and still be willing to destroy the one thing that made her truly happy?"

Chandrika's face softened, her eyes filled with compassion. "Because he believed he was right, Aanya. He thought he was protecting her, keeping her from a life he couldn't understand. In his mind, he was saving her from a future he saw as shameful. But in doing so, he destroyed her."

Aanya looked down, her fists clenched, her chest tight with the weight of betrayal and sorrow. "Did she ever forgive him?"

Chandrika let out a long sigh, her gaze heavy. "Savitri never spoke a word against her brother, never let her bitterness show. But I knew Aanya. I saw the way she looked at him, the pain she buried behind her smile. A part of her heart never healed; a part of her remained with Dev in a place that Neeraj could never touch."

Aanya's voice shook as she asked, "Did she ever talk to him again about it? Did she ever let him see how much he hurt her?"

Chandrika's gaze softened. "Savitri was a woman of quiet strength. She didn't confront him, didn't argue. She accepted the life her family gave her, but she carried that wound for the rest of her life. And when she finally married Rajesh, she did so with grace and dignity, but a part of her was lost forever."

Aanya's tears flowed freely now, her heart heavy with grief for her grandmother's lost love, for the life she had been forced to bury. She looked up at Chandrika, her voice filled with fierce determination. "Thank you for telling me,

Aunty. I needed to know… all of it. Dadi's story deserves to be told, and it deserves the truth."

Chandrika reached out, her hand covering Aanya's. "You are giving her something she was never given, Aanya. You are giving her a voice, a chance to be seen and remembered. She would be proud of you, child."

As Aanya left Chandrika's home, she felt the weight of her family's betrayal pressing down upon her. The love her grandmother had carried, the love she had been forced to bury, had been stripped from her by the very people who should have protected her. And now, Aanya was left to carry that burden, to remember and honour the life her grandmother had been denied.

When she reached the guesthouse, she found Rohan waiting, his face filled with concern as he saw the turmoil in her eyes. Without a word, he opened his arms, and Aanya fell into his embrace, her tears spilling over as she clung to him, the weight of her grief pressing down on her chest.

"They betrayed her, Rohan," she whispered, her voice breaking. "Her own family… they took her love from her. They turned it into something shameful, something she had to hide."

Rohan's arms tightened around her, his voice steady and comforting. "I'm so sorry, Aanya. I can't imagine the pain she must have carried. But you're here now. You're giving her story the dignity it was denied."

Aanya pulled back, looking up at him with tear-filled eyes, her voice choked with a fierce resolve. "I won't let her story be forgotten. I won't let what they did to her be hidden. She deserves to be remembered for who she truly was, for the love she carried, even if it was never given the life it deserved."

Rohan's gaze softened, admiration filling his eyes as he brushed a tear from her cheek. "Then let's make sure her story is told, Aanya."

At that moment, as they stood together, the shadows of betrayal and heartbreak surrounding them, Aanya felt a renewed sense of purpose. She would carry her grandmother's story forward, not as a tale of duty or obedience, but as a story of love, resilience, and quiet defiance.

And as the night settled over Nandipur, Aanya made a silent promise—to honour the untold chapters of Savitri's life, not through sorrow but by carrying forward her spirit of resilience and love, ensuring that her story would never be forgotten.

Letters Beneath the Banyan Tree

The sun rose in muted gold and pinks over Nandipur, casting a soft glow across the village. Aanya's gaze fell on the banyan tree in the distance, its presence steady and unchanging, a silent witness to the stories it had seen unfold. She approached it slowly, her heart heavy with the weight of her grandmother's story. This was the place where Savitri and Dev's paths had crossed, where love had blossomed against all odds. Aanya reached out, letting her fingers brush the rough bark, not for the tree's supposed magic but for the history it held, a history she was now a part of.

Rohan followed closely behind, his usual quiet presence now charged with a sense of reverence. He had been with Aanya through every revelation, each heart-wrenching discovery, and he could feel the significance of this moment as much as she did. This tree, so old and immense, had once been a sacred refuge for her grandmother, a place where love had blossomed and secrets had been exchanged.

Aanya placed her hand on the rough bark of the banyan, her fingers tracing its grooves as though she might find words inscribed there as if Dev and Savitri had carved their love into the tree itself. She let out a shaky breath, looking up at the branches that stretched endlessly, almost seeming to cradle the sky.

"They were here, Rohan," she whispered, her voice tinged with wonder and sorrow. "This was where they could be themselves. This tree, these roots... they witnessed everything."

Rohan stepped closer, his gaze thoughtful as he ran his fingers over the bark beside hers. "Do you think it remembers them? All the love, the promises, the dreams they shared under these branches?"

Aanya's heart tightened, her throat aching with the weight of unspoken hopes. "I don't know," she murmured, "but I hoped... I hoped that if I came here and stood where they stood, I'd feel something. A connection. Maybe even find... some kind of clue."

She glanced down, her voice barely audible. "I feel like I'm looking for ghosts, Rohan. And I don't even know if they're here."

Rohan gave her a reassuring smile, his hand resting on her shoulder. "Then let's look, Aanya. Maybe we'll find something they left behind – a letter, a token… something she never wanted anyone else to find except you."

Aanya nodded, her heart swelling with fragile hope. She knelt down, her hands tracing the roots that sprawled across the ground in thick, twisting lines, like veins feeding life into the earth. Some roots dipped and curved, creating hollows and small pockets that might have held secrets over the years. She felt the soil, her fingers brushing over each crevice as if hoping to touch a piece of her grandmother's life.

Rohan joined her, his gaze serious as he examined each nook and cranny with careful precision. "If she left anything here," he murmured, "it would be somewhere hidden, somewhere only she and Dev knew."

Aanya bit her lip, her fingers trembling as she dug gently around one of the larger roots. She imagined her grandmother sitting here, slipping a letter or a small keepsake between the roots, trusting the tree to keep her secrets safe. "Dadi must have come here with him so many times," she whispered. "It was their sanctuary, a place where they could just… be."

After several minutes, Aanya paused, her hands brushing over a section where two roots curved tightly around each other, forming a small hollow space. The soil there looked softer, slightly disturbed, as though something had once been placed there and then covered over again.

"Rohan," she whispered, her voice barely audible. "I think... there's something here."

Rohan knelt beside her, his eyes widening as he watched her clear away the dirt, her fingers moving with both urgency and reverence. As the soil fell away, she uncovered the corner of a small wooden box, its edges worn and cracked, the wood aged and weathered from years beneath the earth. She held her breath, her heart racing as she carefully lifted the box from the ground.

"Aanya," Rohan murmured, his voice filled with awe. "Do you think...?"

Aanya looked at him, her hands trembling as she wiped away the dust. She felt a surge of anticipation and fear, as though opening the box would bridge the gap between past and present as if she were about to touch something sacred. She carefully lifted the latch, her fingers shaking as she opened the lid.

Inside, nestled on a bed of dried rose petals, was a small bundle of letters tied with a faded red ribbon. The petals, though brittle with age, still held a faint, delicate scent that mingled with the earthy aroma of the soil. Aanya's breath caught in her throat as she read the words written on the topmost letter: *"For my dearest Savitri."*

Her voice trembled as she spoke, barely above a whisper. "These are from Dev... they must be."

Rohan's gaze softened, a gentle smile spreading across his face. "She never told anyone. She hid these away, trusting that maybe, someday, someone would find them. Maybe she hoped it would be you."

Aanya felt tears pricking at her eyes as she untied the ribbon, her fingers brushing over the delicate, looping script. She opened the first letter, her heart pounding as she read the words Dev had written all those years ago, words that seemed to leap across time.

"My dearest Savitri, The world feels colder without you. Each night, I come to this tree, hoping to feel your warmth, your presence. It is here that I leave these words, hoping they will reach you, hoping that, in some way, we are together, even if only through ink and paper. If fate does not allow us life in each other's arms, then let it give us this—a place where our souls can meet, where I can leave pieces of myself for you to find, even if I am gone."

Aanya's voice wavered as she read, her heart breaking for the man who had poured his soul into each line. She closed her eyes, feeling the depth of Dev's love and his longing, as though he were standing beside her, his voice whispering those words in her ear.

She turned to Rohan, her voice choked with emotion. "He came here, night after night, just to leave these letters for her. Even if he couldn't be with her, he found a way to stay connected."

Rohan's hand rested gently on her shoulder. "It's heartbreaking, Aanya. But it's also beautiful. He left a part of himself here, hoping that somehow, in some way, they would always be together."

Aanya took a shaky breath, her fingers tracing the edges of the letter. "She must have come here too. She must have known... even if she couldn't see him, she must have felt his presence, felt the love he left behind."

She carefully unfolded the next letter, the ink slightly smudged, as though Dev's hands had trembled as he wrote.

"Savitri, If you are reading this, know that I am with you, even if only in spirit. I have left pieces of myself here, in this tree, for you to find whenever you need me. I dream of a life with you every night—a life where we are free, where no one can tell us we are wrong. But if I cannot live that life with you, then I will live in these words, in the silence of this tree. I will wait here for you, my love, until the end of time."

Aanya's hands shook as she read, the sorrow and love woven into each word filling her with an ache so deep it felt endless. She looked up at Rohan, her voice barely a whisper. "He left these here, knowing she might never read them. But he did it anyway. He gave her something that even time couldn't erase."

Rohan nodded, his gaze filled with compassion. "He was trying to keep their love alive, even when the world tried to silence it. And now… now that love has reached you, Aanya. You're here, giving voice to everything they endured."

Aanya clutched the letters to her chest, her tears spilling over as she imagined her grandmother discovering these words, perhaps long after Dev had vanished, perhaps when she had come to the tree seeking comfort. "I just… I wish I could have known her like this, Rohan. I wish I could have seen her love, her dreams."

Rohan brushed a tear from her cheek, his voice gentle. "You are seeing her, Aanya. In every letter, in every word he left for her, you're touching her heart. And she wanted you to find this. She trusted you with her story."

Aanya looked down at the letters; the ink faded yet was still alive with emotion. She thought of her grandmother, a woman who had carried a secret love through a life of duty, who had buried her pain but never her heart. "I came here hoping for answers, Rohan, but I found something even more precious. I found her love, the part of her that was never taken."

Aanya gently placed the letters back in the box, closing it with a sense of reverence. She held the box close, her heart brimming with bittersweet joy. "I'm taking this home, Rohan. I'm taking them both home, so that their love can finally be a part of our family's story, a part of us."

Rohan took her hand, his touch warm and steady. "And I'll be right beside you, Aanya, helping you carry it forward."

They lingered beneath the banyan tree, the silence around them filled with the echoes of love and memory. Aanya closed her eyes, sending a silent prayer of gratitude to the spirits of Dev and Savitri, thanking them for leaving behind this part of themselves and for trusting her to find it.

As they made their way back, the sun dipping low over Nandipur, Aanya felt a peace settle over her, a feeling of wholeness she hadn't known she needed. She hadn't found all the answers, hadn't uncovered every piece of the past, but she had found something far greater, a love that had transcended time, a story that would now live on, unbroken and remembered.

And as the gentle warmth of the sun's last rays bathed her face, Aanya knew that her grandmother's spirit would walk with her, guiding her, a love that would endure beyond the silence.

Tides of the Heart

The days in Nandipur had been filled with revelations that seemed to shake the very ground beneath Aanya's feet. Her grandmother's love story, once hidden and silent, had become a part of her own life, intertwining with her emotions and dreams in ways she hadn't anticipated. And amidst this journey into the past, Aanya found herself grappling with an unexpected shift within her, her own heart pulling her toward Rohan, her oldest friend, in a way that left her both elated and unsettled.

She had come to Nandipur hoping to understand her grandmother, to uncover the truth of a love story that had been buried. But now, she was questioning the foundations of her own heart, the boundaries between friendship and love, between duty and desire. The weight of her family's history, the legacy of unfulfilled love and sacrifice, pressed on her in quiet moments, making her question her choices and her path.

One quiet evening, as the sky turned dusky pink, Aanya found herself alone in her small room, her mind swirling with thoughts she could no longer keep to herself. She reached for her phone and dialled Mansi's number, her fingers trembling as she pressed 'call'. Mansi was her oldest friend, her confidante, the one person she trusted to listen without judgement.

After a few rings, Mansi's familiar voice came through, warm and welcoming. "Aanya! It's been ages! How's Nandipur treating you?"

Aanya let out a shaky laugh, a mixture of relief and sadness flooding her. "Mansi... I don't even know where to begin. It's like I've stepped into someone else's life. Every day here feels like I'm uncovering something new, and it's beautiful, but... it's also overwhelming."

Mansi's tone softened, her voice filled with understanding. "It sounds like you're carrying a lot. Tell me, Aanya. What's on your mind?"

Aanya hesitated, trying to find the words. "I came here to understand Dadi's story, to learn about this love she never shared with us. And I have, Mansi. I've found letters and places she and Dev shared. I feel like I know her in ways I never did before. But it's complicated because... because I'm not just learning about her; I'm learning about myself. And I'm not sure I like everything I'm finding."

Mansi stayed silent, giving her the space to continue. Aanya took a deep breath, her voice filled with vulnerability. "The more I uncover about her life, the more I question everything: my family, my identity... even my own feelings. It's as if her story has opened this part of me I didn't know existed."

Mansi's voice was soft but encouraging. "That sounds powerful, Aanya. But tell me, what exactly are you questioning?"

Aanya's heart pounded, her words spilling out faster than she could control. "I'm questioning... myself. Who I am and who I want to be. And then there's Rohan." She paused, her breath catching at the thought of him. "Being here with him, going through all of this together... it's changing things between us, Mansi. I thought he was just my friend, but now... I don't know what he is to me anymore."

Mansi let out a soft laugh, a knowing smile in her voice. "Ah, so the pieces are finally falling into place. I've been waiting for you to see this, Aanya."

Aanya's cheeks flushed, even though Mansi couldn't see her. "Mansi, it's not that simple. We've known each other our whole lives. He's... he's Rohan. And I don't even know if he feels the same. And even if he does, I don't know if I can let myself feel this way."

Mansi's voice softened, filled with warmth. "Aanya, you're carrying a lot of weight and a lot of family history, which is making you question everything. But don't let the past dictate your future. You're not your grandmother, and this isn't her story. It's yours."

Aanya let out a sigh, her mind spinning with the implications. "But that's just it, Mansi. How can I even think… about loving someone when my grandmother's story ended in heartbreak? She sacrificed everything and buried her love for the sake of family and duty. And now, here I am, thinking about my own happiness, wondering if I even have the right to… to feel this way for Rohan."

Mansi's voice grew firmer, her words laced with encouragement. "Aanya, your grandmother didn't leave her story for you to repeat it. She left it for you to learn from, to understand her, yes, but also to let go of the burdens she had to carry. Don't chain yourself to her past, to her sacrifices. If she could see you now, do you think she'd want you to hold back from happiness?"

Aanya's heart ached, her throat tightening. "I want to believe that, Mansi. But it feels like such a betrayal. Like if I let myself love him, I'm erasing her pain, her struggles."

Mansi's voice softened, filled with empathy. "Aanya, honouring her memory doesn't mean recreating her pain. If anything, it means freeing yourself from it. Let yourself love, not because she couldn't, but because she'd want you to."

Aanya wiped a tear from her cheek, her voice barely a whisper. "You really think so?"

"I know so," Mansi replied, her tone filled with certainty. "You don't have to let the past define you. Rohan isn't just a part of this journey; he's been by your side through every discovery and every revelation. Maybe it's time to let him be a part of your story, not just as a friend, but as... something more."

Aanya's heart swelled with both fear and hope, her voice tinged with uncertainty. "But what if... what if it doesn't work out? What if I let myself feel this, and then I lose him?"

Mansi's laughter was soft and comforting. "Then you'll have loved. Isn't that what life is, Aanya? Taking the risk, allowing yourself to be vulnerable, to feel deeply, even if it doesn't come with guarantees?"

Aanya sighed, a small smile tugging at her lips. "When did you become so wise?"

Mansi chuckled. "I've been listening to you grapple with everyone's emotions for years, Aanya. I've learned a thing or two. But seriously... talk to him. Let him know how you feel, bit by bit. You don't have to rush it, and you don't have to have all the answers right now."

Aanya nodded, her heart calming, clarity settling over her like a gentle breeze. "Thank you, Mansi. I didn't realise how much I needed to hear that."

Mansi's voice softened, filled with warmth. "Anytime, Aanya. And remember, this is your story. No one else's. You have every right to write it the way you want."

Aanya ended the call, her mind clearer, her heart steadier. She looked out of her window at the village, the soft glow of the evening casting a peaceful aura over Nandipur. Somewhere out there, Rohan was waiting, probably with that patient smile that never failed to calm her, that look in his eyes that had lately started to mean so much more than friendship.

She took a deep breath, feeling the truth settle in her chest. Her grandmother's story, as beautiful and tragic as it was, didn't have to be hers. And as much as she would honour Savitri's memory, she also had the right to live her own life and follow her own heart.

Rohan had become a part of her journey more than she had ever anticipated. And perhaps, just perhaps, he was meant to be a part of her future, as her own new beginning.

And with a steady heart, Aanya realised that the legacy she wanted to carry wasn't one of quiet resignation, but one of love, of courage, of choosing her own path, no matter where it might lead.

Strength in Resolve

A anya lay awake in her room as the first light of dawn filtered through the window, casting a soft, golden hue across the walls. She stared at the ceiling, her mind buzzing with the fragments of her grandmother's life that she had pieced together. The more she uncovered about Dadi's story, the more she realised that this journey was as much about her own growth as it was about understanding her grandmother's past. She knew that she couldn't leave Nandipur until she had uncovered everything, even if it meant facing difficult truths.

Sitting up, Aanya felt a sense of quiet resolve settle over her – a calmness born from the knowledge that she was where she was meant to be, on a path that her grandmother had unknowingly set for her. The questions she carried were not just about the past but were tied to her own heart, to her own understanding of love, duty, and identity.

After a quick breakfast, she found Rohan waiting for her in the small garden behind the guesthouse. He was sitting on a low stone wall, his camera in hand, studying the morning light as it played across the leaves. When he noticed her, he lowered the camera, his face breaking into a warm smile that seemed to dissolve some of the tension she felt.

"Good morning," he greeted, his voice gentle yet filled with curiosity. "You look... different today. Determined."

Aanya returned his smile, feeling a surge of gratitude for his unwavering presence. "Good morning, Rohan. I guess you're right. I woke up with this sense that I couldn't leave until I knew everything. Until I know what happened to Dev... and what Dadi's life truly meant."

Rohan tilted his head, studying her intently. "You're carrying a lot, Aanya. But I think you're stronger than you realise. And I'm here, whatever you need."

She felt her heart warm at his words, his support grounding her in a way she couldn't quite describe. "I couldn't have come this far without you, Rohan. Every time I feel like giving up, like I'll never find the answers, you're there, reminding me why this matters. And I... I don't know how to thank you for that."

Rohan's smile softened, his gaze filled with understanding. "Aanya, you don't have to thank me. I'm here because I believe in you and because some stories deserve to be heard. Your grandmother's story, your story… they deserve that."

Aanya looked down, feeling the weight of his words settle over her. She took a deep breath, her resolve hardening. "You're right. Dadi's story deserves to be known, even if it's painful, even if it's messy. I can't leave until I understand every part of her life, even the parts she never spoke of."

Rohan placed a comforting hand on her shoulder, his voice steady. "Then let's find those answers together. Whatever it takes."

Aanya nodded, her mind racing as she considered her next steps. The letters they had found beneath the banyan tree had given her a glimpse into the depth of her grandmother's love for Dev, but they hadn't answered the questions that gnawed at her – the mystery of Dev's disappearance, the reason her grandmother had carried her sorrow in silence.

"What's our next step?" Rohan asked, breaking the silence, his tone light but his eyes serious.

Aanya thought carefully, her mind flashing to the conversation they had with Inspector Deshmukh, the retired officer who had hinted at secrets left unsaid. "Inspector Deshmukh," she murmured, her voice thoughtful. "He told us that Dev's body was never found and that there were suspicions surrounding his disappearance. But he didn't tell us everything. I have a feeling he knows more than he's letting on."

Rohan's eyes brightened, understanding dawning on his face. "You think he could be holding back? Maybe there's something he wasn't ready to share with us."

Aanya nodded, determination flashing in her eyes. "Yes. I think he was trying to protect us or maybe protect himself. But I need to know. I've come too far to stop now."

They set out later that morning, following the winding path that led to Inspector Deshmukh's modest home on the outskirts of the village. The road was quiet, bordered by lush fields and dense clusters of trees that swayed gently in the morning breeze. The air was thick with the smell of rain, a storm brewing on the horizon, mirroring the tension in Aanya's heart.

When they reached the inspector's home, Aanya hesitated for a moment, steeling herself before knocking on the door. Moments later, the door creaked open, and Inspector Deshmukh appeared, his expression surprised but not unwelcoming.

"Aanya... Rohan," he greeted, his voice laced with curiosity. "I wasn't expecting to see you both this morning."

Aanya offered a small, polite smile, her voice steady as she spoke. "I'm sorry to come by unannounced, Inspector, but I have more questions. About Dev... about my grandmother. I feel there's more to the story, more than you've shared with us. And I... I need to know the truth."

Inspector Deshmukh studied her for a moment, his gaze flickering with something unreadable. But after a brief hesitation, he stepped aside, gesturing for them to enter. They followed him into his small sitting room, the walls adorned with faded photographs and remnants of a life lived in quiet service.

Once they were seated, Aanya took a deep breath, her heart pounding as she prepared to speak. "Inspector, you told me that Dev's body was never found and that there were suspicions. I need to know what people thought back then and what you think happened to him. Please... my grandmother deserves for her story to be known."

The inspector's gaze softened, his eyes shadowed by years of unspoken truths. He leaned forward, his voice quiet, his tone heavy. "Aanya, I understand your need for answers. But you must know much of what happened to Dev remains shrouded in mystery. I don't even have all the pieces. But..." He paused as if weighing his words carefully. "There were whispers in the village, suspicions that Dev's own family may have played a role in his disappearance."

Aanya felt a chill run down her spine, her heart pounding as his words sank in. "You think... you think his family might have... hurt him?"

Inspector Deshmukh nodded slowly, his expression grim. "I don't know for certain, Aanya. But Dev's father, Dhaniram Malhotra, was a strict, prideful man. He valued his family's honour above all else, and when he discovered Dev's relationship with Savitri, he was enraged. To him, Dev's love was a disgrace, a stain on the family's name. And Dev... he was a determined young man, unafraid to stand up to his father."

Aanya felt tears pricking at her eyes as she imagined Dev, a young man filled with love and conviction, standing up to his father for the woman he cherished. She looked at the inspector, her voice barely a whisper. "And my grandmother... did she ever know about these suspicions? Did she ever suspect that Dev's family... might have harmed him?"

The inspector's gaze softened, his expression tinged with sadness. "Your grandmother came to me once, a few weeks after Dev disappeared. She asked if there was any chance he was alive and if he might have left the village to escape his father's anger. I could see the hope in her eyes, even though... even though she must have known, deep down, that he was gone."

Aanya's heart ached as she imagined her grandmother waiting for a love that would never return, carrying the weight of that loss in silence. She blinked back tears, her voice thick with sorrow. "Thank you, Inspector... thank you for sharing this with me."

Inspector Deshmukh nodded, his expression filled with compassion. "Aanya, your grandmother was a remarkable woman, filled with strength and grace. She carried her love for Dev with her, even in silence. And now, you're here, carrying her story forward. Don't let it go unfinished."

As they left the inspector's home, Aanya felt a wave of determination settles over her, a quiet but unbreakable resolve. She had come to Nandipur seeking understanding, but now she knew she was on a journey to honour her grandmother's life, her sacrifices, and her love. She couldn't leave until she had uncovered every piece of the story, no matter how painful or difficult.

Rohan walked beside her, his presence steady and grounding. When they were out of earshot, he turned to her, his gaze filled with warmth and support. "Aanya, you don't have to carry this alone. I'm here for whatever you need."

Aanya looked at him, her heart swelling with gratitude, her voice filled with quiet strength. "Thank you, Rohan. I couldn't have done this without you. And... I'm not giving up. I'm going to keep going until I understand everything until my grandmother's story is whole."

Rohan smiled, his eyes bright with admiration. "Then let's keep going. We'll honour her story together."

As they walked back to the guesthouse, Aanya felt a renewed sense of purpose, a clarity that she hadn't felt before. She was no longer simply uncovering a family mystery; she was fighting to bring a voice to a love that had been silenced, to honour a legacy that had been buried for too long. She knew there would be more obstacles and more moments of doubt, but with Rohan by her side and the fire in her heart, she was ready to face whatever lay ahead.

For the first time, Aanya felt like she truly understood what her grandmother would have wanted. Not for her story to be retold as a tragedy, but as a testament to resilience, to the kind of love that could survive even in silence. And as she looked towards the village, the sun casting a warm glow over the rooftops, she knew she was exactly where she was meant to be.

Her journey was far from over, but with every step, she was carrying her grandmother's love forward, giving it life in a way that felt both timeless and true.

Race Against Time

T he news came unexpectedly, a rumour that spread quickly through the narrow lanes of Nandipur, whispered in hushed voices and punctuated with worried glances. Aanya and Rohan had been walking through the bustling village square when they overheard two elderly men discussing the upcoming demolition of the old Malhotra haveli. Aanya's heart sank at their words, her mind racing with the implications.

"Rohan," she whispered, her voice tight with urgency, "did you hear that? They're planning to demolish Dev's haveli, the place where he lived and where his family kept so many secrets. If they tear it down, any evidence of his life, his fate… it could be lost forever."

Rohan's face mirrored her concern, his eyes wide with alarm. "Aanya, we need to go there now. If there's anything left, anything that could give us answers, we have to find it before it's too late."

Without another word, they turned and hurried through the narrow streets, past the brightly painted houses and the market stalls where vendors called out to passersby. Aanya's heart pounded with a mix of fear and urgency. She knew this might be her last chance to uncover the truth about Dev, her last chance to find the missing pieces of her grandmother's story.

As they approached the haveli, Aanya's breath caught in her throat. The old mansion stood like a fading monument, its once-grand facade weathered by time, the paint peeling and the stone cracked. The windows were dark and empty, and the garden, once lush, had become overgrown with wild vines and weeds. Yet even in its dilapidated state, the haveli exuded a quiet dignity, a sense of the lives and memories that had once filled its walls.

Rohan placed a reassuring hand on her shoulder, his voice steady. "Are you ready for this, Aanya?"

She took a deep breath, steeling herself. "Yes, I have to be."

They approached the entrance, pushing open the heavy wooden doors with a creak that echoed through the empty halls. Inside, the air was thick with dust, the scent of aged wood and mildew permeating the space. Sunlight streamed through the cracked windows, casting shadows that danced across the floor, creating an eerie, almost otherworldly atmosphere.

Aanya ran her fingers along the walls as they walked, feeling a strange connection to the place where Dev had once lived, where her grandmother's love had blossomed in secret. She could almost picture Dev as a young man, moving through these very halls, his heart filled with dreams that had been torn apart by forces beyond his control.

They entered what must have been the main sitting room, the walls lined with old paintings and the furniture draped in faded, tattered sheets. Rohan moved to examine a dusty cabinet in the corner, his voice barely a whisper. "Do you think there's anything here, Aanya? Anything that might tell us what happened to him?"

Aanya bit her lip, her gaze scanning the room. "I don't know. But there has to be something, some trace of him... something that his family didn't destroy or hide away."

They moved through the house methodically, checking each room, each drawer, each forgotten corner. The silence was heavy, broken only by the creak of floorboards and the soft rustle of their footsteps. Aanya's heart raced with each discovery – a yellowed newspaper, a broken trinket, a dusty mirror that seemed to reflect her own sense of longing.

Finally, they reached what appeared to be a study, a small room tucked away at the back of the house. The walls were lined with bookshelves, their contents untouched, as though time itself had preserved this one room. A large wooden desk sat in the centre, its surface covered with papers that had long since faded. Aanya approached it cautiously, her fingers brushing over the brittle pages.

"Look," Rohan said, pointing to a drawer in the desk. "Maybe there's something inside."

Aanya knelt down, pulling at the drawer. It was stuck, the wood swollen with age, but with a bit of effort, it finally gave way, revealing a small bundle of papers tied together with a piece of fraying twine. She lifted them carefully, her hands trembling as she examined the top sheet.

It was a letter written in an elegant, looping script that was both familiar and foreign. The words were faded but legible enough to read. The seal on the envelope was still intact, a silent testament to words written but never seen, emotions poured onto paper yet never shared.

"Dear Dev,

I cannot continue to watch you bring shame upon our family. Your foolish attachment to that girl has become a stain on our honour, a weakness that you cannot afford. I have given you every chance to put this behind you, but you refuse. If you do not end this... if you do not break free from this attachment, there will be consequences, consequences you cannot escape."

Aanya's heart twisted as she read the words, the coldness, the cruelty evident in every line. She could feel the weight of Dhaniram Malhotra's disapproval, the iron grip he had held over Dev's life, forcing him to choose between his family's honour and the woman he loved.

Rohan's expression mirrored his shock as he read over her shoulder. "Aanya... this letter. It's a threat. Dev's father was willing to go to any lengths to keep him away from your grandmother."

Aanya swallowed, her voice barely a whisper. "It's more than that, Rohan. This letter... it's proof that his family might have been involved in his disappearance, that they might have... might have done something to make him disappear."

She clutched the papers to her chest, her heart racing with a mix of fear and desperation. "If they demolish this place, Rohan, any evidence, any traces of Dev's life and what happened to him could be lost forever."

Rohan placed a comforting hand on her shoulder, his voice steady and grounded. "Then we won't let that happen. We'll document everything we find here. If this is all we have left of his life, then we'll make sure it's not forgotten."

Aanya nodded, determination hardening within her. "We need to hurry. There could be more letters, more clues about what really happened."

They combed through the rest of the room, uncovering a few more scattered notes, each one echoing the tension, the impossible choice Dev had faced. Each piece of paper felt like a glimpse into his inner turmoil and his desire to be with Savitri even as his family closed in around him, leaving him no escape.

At last, they found a small leather-bound journal, its cover worn and scuffed, the edges softened with use. Aanya opened it, her breath catching as she read the first few lines. It was Dev's journal, filled with entries that spoke of his love for Savitri, his dreams of a life with her, and his anguish as the walls of his family's expectations closed in around him.

"They do not understand what she means to me, nor do they care. To them, she is a distraction, an inconvenience, something to be erased. But she is my life, my heart. Without her, I am nothing. I would rather be exiled from my family, from this village, than live a life without her by my side."

Aanya's fingers brushed against the edges of the diary as she turned the page, her breath hitching at the next line. Her eyes lingered on the ink as though willing herself to absorb the emotions woven into the words. She paused, her chest tightening with an ache she couldn't name. She set the diary down for a moment, staring into the distance as if trying to bridge the gap between her grandmother's life and her own. She could feel Dev's love, his desperation, and his desire to escape the chains of tradition and find freedom with her grandmother. But she also sensed his fear, his awareness that his family would never let him go so easily.

Rohan's hand found hers, a steady presence grounding her. "He loved her, Aanya. Even when the world tried to keep them apart, he held on to that love. And now, through this journal, he's given you a piece of himself, a truth that can't be silenced."

Aanya looked up at him, her eyes filled with tears. "Rohan... what if this is all we ever find? What if we never know exactly what happened to him, why he disappeared?"

Rohan's gaze softened, his voice gentle. "Then we honour him by preserving what we do know. By keeping his words, his love, alive. And maybe... maybe that's enough."

Aanya took a deep breath, clutching the journal tightly. She knew that the full story of her grandmother's love and loss might never be uncovered and that some questions would remain unanswered. But in this journal, in the letters and papers they had found, she had glimpsed the truth of Dev's heart, the love that had been buried beneath silence and secrecy.

As they left the haveli, Aanya cast one last look back at the crumbling walls, the shadows that had hidden so many memories. She could feel the weight of Dev's presence, the spirit of a man who had loved fiercely, who had defied his family and his fate, even if only in his heart.

Walking away, she felt a renewed sense of purpose, a promise to carry forward the legacy of that love, to share the truth of her grandmother's story so that it might never be forgotten, even if the haveli itself were reduced to dust.

And as she looked at Rohan beside her, she knew that she wasn't alone on this journey, that the love she was honouring was guiding her, lighting the path forward, a path that was as much hers as it was Dev and Savitri's.

Uncovering the Past

The decision was made quickly, almost without words. The next morning, Aanya and Rohan went straight to Inspector Deshmukh's modest home, their hearts filled with urgency. If the haveli was to be demolished soon, they couldn't afford to waste another moment. They needed as many eyes and as much expertise as possible to help them uncover whatever secrets the old mansion held.

When they reached his door, Aanya knocked, her hands trembling with anticipation. Inspector Deshmukh answered with a look of surprise, his brow furrowing as he saw their expressions.

"Inspector," Aanya began, her voice steady despite her racing heart. "We need your help. The Malhotra haveli is about to be demolished, and... we think there may be clues there, evidence about what really happened to Dev."

Inspector Deshmukh studied her face, his eyes narrowing slightly. "The old Malhotra haveli, you say? It's been abandoned for years. What makes you think there might still be something there?"

Aanya took a deep breath, choosing her words carefully. "We've already found letters and a journal that belonged to Dev. His father left behind some... threatening words, demanding that he end his relationship with my grandmother. We believe there could be more, something that might finally tell us what happened to him."

The inspector's expression softened, a look of understanding settling over him. "I see. You want to gather whatever you can before it's all lost to time."

Aanya nodded, her voice filled with determination. "Yes. I need to know the truth, Inspector. My grandmother deserves that, and so does Dev."

After a moment's pause, he sighed and nodded, grabbing his hat and jacket from a nearby hook. "Very well. Let's go. If there's anything left, I'll do my best to help you find it."

The three of them made their way through the winding streets of Nandipur, the early morning quiet adding a sense of solemnity to their journey. When they reached the haveli, its crumbling facade loomed before them like a spectre from the past, a relic of a story that had been left unfinished for far too long.

Inside, the air was thick with dust, the faint scent of decay lingering in the corners. The inspector moved with a practised eye, scanning the room with the precision of someone who had spent years noticing details others might overlook.

"Where did you find the letters and journal?" he asked, his voice low.

"In a drawer in the study," Aanya replied, leading him to the small, dimly lit room at the back of the house. "We searched as thoroughly as we could, but... I thought maybe you'd see something we missed."

The inspector knelt down by the desk, carefully inspecting each drawer, each corner of the room. He ran his fingers along the edges, tapping gently to check for hollow spaces. Rohan watched him with admiration, impressed by the old man's meticulousness.

After a few minutes, Inspector Deshmukh's hand stilled over a section of the wooden panelling beneath the desk. He pressed against it, a faint click echoing in the silence. A small compartment slid open, revealing a hidden space lined with papers, yellowed with age.

"Looks like we found something," he murmured, glancing up at Aanya and Rohan with a hint of a smile.

Aanya's breath caught as she peered into the compartment, her heart racing. Inside were several folded documents, along with a small leather pouch that seemed to contain something heavy. She reached out, her fingers trembling as she lifted the pouch and gently opened it. Inside was a tarnished silver locket with the initials 'D.S.' engraved on the back. She held it up, her voice barely a whisper.

"Dev's locket... the one he always wore," she murmured, her mind flashing to her grandmother's stories of the young man who had once captivated her heart. "He never went anywhere without it."

Rohan leaned in, studying the locket. "Aanya, if this locket was left here, it means he might not have left willingly. It's almost as if he was... forced to abandon it."

Aanya's eyes widened, realisation dawning on her. "This locket was precious to him. If he was leaving on his own, he would have taken it. This means he might not have had a choice."

Inspector Deshmukh nodded gravely, his expression thoughtful. "It's possible that his family... or someone else close to him... ensured he never returned."

The inspector's words hung in the air, and Aanya felt a wave of grief wash over her. She had spent so long imagining her grandmother's love story as one of the stolen glances and whispered promises, but now she was beginning to understand the darker side of that love, the sacrifices, the betrayals, and the heartbreak that had remained hidden.

As they continued searching, Rohan noticed a stack of letters tucked beneath a broken floorboard near the corner of the room. He knelt down, carefully pulling out the bundle, the paper fragile and faded.

"More letters," he said, holding them out to Aanya. "These might be from Dev to Savitri. They look just like the ones we found under the banyan tree."

Aanya took the letters, her heart pounding as she unfolded the top one. The handwriting was unmistakable, Dev's elegant script, each word filled with the passion and longing he had carried for her grandmother.

"Savitri,

I fear that my days are numbered. My father's anger grows with each passing day, and he has made it clear that there is no room for compromise. I am being watched and monitored at every turn. I wish I could be with you, that I could hold you and promise you the life we dreamed of. But if I cannot, know this: you are my heart, my soul. I will carry you with me, wherever I am, in this life and beyond."

Aanya's hands shook as she read the letter, tears filling her eyes. This wasn't just a love story, it was a tragedy. Dev had known his life was in danger, had known that his family would go to any lengths to stop him from being with her grandmother. And yet, he had continued to love her, to fight for her, even if only in his heart.

Rohan placed a comforting hand on her shoulder, his voice soft. "Aanya... he loved her until the very end. Even when he knew he was in danger, he held on to that love."

Aanya nodded, swallowing the lump in her throat. "And Dadi never knew... she never knew how much he had risked for her, how deeply he had loved her."

Inspector Deshmukh continued to search the room, his gaze falling on a small, locked box hidden beneath a stack of papers in the corner. He lifted it carefully, turning it over in his hands. "It appears to be locked, but I believe I can open it with a little effort."

Aanya watched, her heart pounding as the inspector worked on the lock. After a few moments, there was a soft click, and the box opened, revealing a few more documents, along with a small notebook bound in black leather. Aanya leaned forward, her breath catching as she realised what it was.

"It's... it's a record," she whispered, flipping through the pages. "It looks like a diary, but it's more... methodical. Notes on Dev's movements, his meetings, even the places he went when he was alone."

The inspector's face darkened, a look of understanding dawning on him. "This was a record kept by someone who was watching him. Someone who wanted to keep track of every aspect of his life."

Rohan's expression turned grim. "His family must have been monitoring him, following him wherever he went. They wanted to make sure he didn't see your grandmother."

Aanya's voice shook as she read aloud one of the entries. *"Today, Dev spent an hour beneath the banyan tree. He appeared to be waiting for someone, but he left before anyone arrived. He must be reminded that his actions have consequences."*

The words were chilling, filled with an underlying menace that sent a shiver down Aanya's spine. This was more than disapproval; it was control and surveillance that bordered on obsession.

"They never let him breathe," she whispered, her voice choked with emotion. "They watched his every move, ensuring that he had no chance to escape, no chance to be with her."

Inspector Deshmukh closed the box, his expression grave. "Aanya, this confirms that Dev was under constant pressure and that his family was determined to break him. They left him no choice. And if he ever tried to defy them… they might have ensured he never returned."

Aanya clutched the letters and the notebook to her chest, her heart heavy with sorrow and anger. Aanya opened the diary once more, her fingers trembling as she turned to a page marked with faint smudges of ink, as if tears had once fallen there. Her eyes scanned the words, her grandmother's voice coming alive through the delicate script:

"There are nights when I sit beneath the banyan tree, the moonlight sifting through its branches, and I imagine what life might have been if things had been different. Suppose love alone had been enough. But I learned long ago that love, no matter how pure, cannot always conquer the world we live in. Still, I held onto it, as fiercely as one holds onto a dying flame, even when the world demanded I let it go."

Aanya's breath caught as she closed the diary and tried to imagine herself in her grandmother's place, watching Dev walk away, powerless to change what was already written. She pictured the loneliness that must have clung to Savitri, the silent strength it must have taken to live on. Aanya clenched the diary tightly, whispering softly, "I'll honour this, Dadi. Your love wasn't in vain."

As they left the haveli, Aanya took one last look back, her eyes filled with a mixture of grief and resolution. The mansion might be torn down, its secrets buried beneath rubble and dust, but she had uncovered enough to piece together the truth, to understand the pain and resilience of her grandmother's love.

With Rohan and Inspector Deshmukh by her side, she knew that she wasn't alone in carrying forward this legacy, in honouring the love that had been silenced for so long.

As they walked away, she felt a new strength within her, a promise to herself and to her grandmother that she would never let this story be forgotten.

Heartfelt Reckoning

The evening air was thick with the scent of jasmine as Aanya sat alone on the terrace of the guesthouse, staring out over the darkening village. The discoveries of the day lingered heavily in her mind: the letters, Dev's locket, and the painful secrets embedded in the old haveli. Each revelation had brought her closer to understanding her grandmother's past, but it had also left her with a growing ache, a feeling of betrayal she hadn't known she was carrying. So much had been hidden, not only from her but from generations before her, and she knew that it was time to bring everything into the light.

As the sky shifted to deeper hues of purple, her phone rang. Aanya glanced at the screen, her heart skipping a beat as she saw her mother's name. She hadn't spoken to Meera in days, uncertain of how to bridge the gap between the woman she had known all her life and the history she had uncovered in Nandipur.

Taking a steadying breath, she answered the call. "Hi, Mom."

"Aanya, beta," Meera's voice was warm, yet there was an edge of concern in it. "I've been worried. It's been so long since you called. Are you... are you all right?"

Aanya hesitated, her heart pounding as she grappled with the emotions swirling inside her. She had come to Nandipur seeking answers, and she had found them, but those answers had brought with them a new understanding of her mother, her family, and the weight of unspoken pain that they all carried.

"Mom, there's... there's a lot we need to talk about," Aanya began, her voice soft but steady. "I've found things here, about Dadi, about Dev. Things that no one ever told me. Things that I think... maybe you didn't know either."

Meera was silent for a moment, and when she spoke again, her voice was filled with tension that matched Aanya's own. "What do you mean, Aanya? What have you found?"

Aanya took a deep breath, trying to keep her emotions in check. "I found letters, Mom. Letters from Dev to Dadi. They loved each other deeply, but his family... threatened him and controlled him. They wouldn't let him be with her. I think... I think they might have even hurt him to keep them apart."

Meera let out a slow, shaky breath on the other end of the line. "Aanya... I didn't know. I knew they loved each other, yes, but I didn't know it was like that. I didn't know the extent of what they went through."

Aanya's voice quivered as she continued, the pain of everything she had uncovered spilling over. "But, Mom, that's not all. Dadi carried that love with her, in silence, her whole life. She raised us, she loved us, but a part of her was always with him. And you... you must have felt that, too. You must have known that she was holding back, that there was a part of her that was... unreachable."

Meera's voice softened, a hint of sadness seeping into her tone. "I did, Aanya. I think I always knew. Dadi was a wonderful mother, but there was a sadness in her, a quietness that I could never fully understand. Sometimes I resented it, even though I didn't want to. I wanted her to be whole, to be fully ours, but I couldn't shake the feeling that she was... haunted by something—or someone—I would never know."

Aanya felt a lump form in her throat, her own anger and sorrow mingling with her mother's. "Why didn't you ever ask her, Mom? Why did you let her carry that burden alone?"

Meera's voice broke slightly, her words filled with regret. "Because I was afraid. Afraid of what I would hear, afraid that if I asked, she would pull away even more.

I wanted to protect her, but in doing so... I think I just pushed her further into herself."

Aanya closed her eyes, a tear slipping down her cheek. "I understand now, Mom. I understand why she was the way she was, why she chose silence. But it hurts, knowing that she loved someone so deeply and never had the chance to live that love. And it makes me wonder... if that's our fate, too. To hold back, to let love slip away because of fear, because of duty."

There was a long pause on the other end, and then Meera's voice softened, filled with a mix of love and sadness. "Aanya, you are not bound to Dadi's choices. You don't have to carry her pain as your own. She made sacrifices, yes, but she also lived with grace and strength. You... you have a choice, Aanya. Don't let her silence become your silence, too."

Aanya took a shaky breath, her thoughts drifting to Rohan. He had been there for her through every step of this journey, supporting her with a quiet strength that felt like a balm to her heart. But her own fear, her uncertainty about repeating her family's legacy of restrained love, had held her back.

"Mom... there's something else," she said her voice barely a whisper. "Rohan... he's been with me this whole time. He's helped me, listened to me, held me together. And I... I think I love him."

Meera was silent for a moment, and when she spoke, her voice was filled with a gentleness that surprised Aanya. "And does that scare you, Aanya?"

Aanya nodded, even though her mother couldn't see her. "Yes. It scares me because I keep thinking about Dadi, about the love she couldn't live, and I wonder if... if maybe I'm not allowed to feel this if I should hold back."

Meera's voice was soft but resolute. "Aanya, your Dadi's story is hers alone. You don't have to repeat her sacrifices. I think... I think she would want you to live freely, to love without fear. If Rohan means something to you, don't hold back. Don't let the weight of our family's history stop you from living your life."

Aanya's heart swelled at her mother's words, a warmth spreading through her that felt like acceptance, like the breaking of a cycle she hadn't even realised she was part of. She wiped away a tear, her voice filled with gratitude. "Thank you, Mom. I needed to hear that. I needed to know that I'm allowed to choose my own path."

Meera's voice was choked with emotion. "Aanya, I may not have understood your Dadi fully, but I know she would want you to be happy. She would want you to embrace love, to live without the shadows that haunted her. And as your mother, I want that for you too."

Aanya closed her eyes, her heart feeling lighter than it had in days. "I promise, Mom. I'll live fully. I'll honour Dadi's memory, but I'll also honour myself, my own life."

A pause lingered between them, filled with unspoken words, an understanding that went beyond anything they had shared before. In that silence, they acknowledged the pain, the love, and the resilience that had shaped their family, the sacrifices made, the hopes left unspoken.

As they ended the call, Aanya felt a sense of resolution wash over her. She stood there on the terrace, the village stretched out below her, the stars beginning to emerge in the night sky. And as she looked toward the horizon, she felt a quiet certainty settle in her heart. Her grandmother's love and her family's sacrifices – they were part of her, yes, but they did not define her.

And now, with Rohan waiting for her below, she felt ready to embrace her future, to let love in, to live fully, not as a shadow of the past but as the woman she was, with a heart wide open.

The Secret Room

The air was thick with anticipation as Aanya, Rohan, and Inspector Deshmukh made their way towards the haveli for what might be their final visit. Rumours had circulated through the village for years about a hidden room somewhere within the Malhotra family's ancestral home, a place said to hold secrets that had been carefully guarded for generations. Aanya felt a shiver of excitement and dread mingle as they approached. If the room existed, it might contain the answers she had travelled so far to find.

Stepping inside the haveli, Aanya felt an odd stillness descend around them. The dim light filtering through the broken windows cast an eerie glow over the hall, making the dust dance in the air like restless spirits. She took a steadying breath, feeling as if she were on the edge of something monumental, something that could reshape her understanding of her grandmother's story forever.

"Are you sure you're okay with this, Aanya?" Rohan's voice was soft and steady as he reached out to touch her hand with a quiet gesture of support.

Aanya nodded, forcing herself to breathe deeply. "I have to be. For Dadi… and for Dev. If there's any part of their story left hidden, I need to bring it to light."

Inspector Deshmukh took the lead, his gaze scanning the walls and floors with a practised eye. They moved carefully through the old rooms, each one bearing faint echoes of the life that had once filled them. After what felt like hours of searching, they came to a small, windowless hallway on the ground floor. Deshmukh paused, his hand hovering over a section of the wall that seemed out of place, a slightly newer panel, as though someone had attempted to conceal something behind it.

"Here," he murmured, pressing his fingers along the seam. A faint clicking sound echoed through the silence, and a section of the wall shifted, revealing a narrow, dark doorway leading down into the depths of the haveli.

Aanya's heart pounded, a mix of fear and exhilaration coursing through her. She felt Rohan's reassuring grip on her shoulder, his steady gaze meeting hers. Together, they stepped into the darkness, descending a flight of narrow stairs that seemed to spiral down endlessly, carrying them deeper into shadows untouched by the outside world.

At the bottom, they found themselves in a small, hidden room. The air was damp and stale, heavy with the scent of age and secrets long buried. In the dim light, Aanya could make out a dusty wooden table at the centre of the room, surrounded by old trunks and boxes piled against the walls. Her attention was drawn to a single item on the table – a letter, yellowed with age, the edges brittle and faded.

With trembling hands, Aanya reached for the letter. The seal was still intact, a silent testament to words written but never read. She unfolded it carefully, her heart racing as she began to read Dev's words, his looping script bringing his voice to life across the years.

"My dearest Savitri,

If fate has led you to this letter, then perhaps a miracle has occurred, allowing me, if only through these words, to reach across time and speak to you once more. I write this, knowing our love might remain buried in silence, a dream half-lived but cherished all the same. My love, I am alive. I could not stay in Nandipur, where our love would bring you only sorrow. So I chose to disappear, to leave without a trace, carrying your memory with every step."

A sob escaped Aanya's lips, her hand flying to her mouth as she absorbed the weight of his words. Her grandmother's love had not been cut short by tragedy but rather by a painful choice–a choice Dev had made to protect her.

"Oh, Dev…" she whispered, her voice thick with emotion. "He left to protect her, to let her have a life free of shame and judgement."

Rohan's hand rested on her shoulder, his voice filled with quiet admiration. "He loved her so deeply that he was willing to disappear into the shadows just so she could live in peace."

Inspector Deshmukh nodded, his gaze fixed on the letter. "It seems he carried her memory with him, choosing to live in silence and solitude rather than risk bringing harm to the woman he loved."

Aanya's tears fell freely as she continued reading, each word laden with Dev's raw, aching love – a love he had carried into exile.

"*Savitri, I have built a life from shadows, carrying you with me in every heartbeat, every breath. In moments of stillness, I imagine the life we might have shared, and I find solace in knowing that, somewhere, you are happy. Know this: you have been and always will be my light in the darkness. If I am never able to hold you again, let this be my legacy to you – a love that even distance and silence cannot erase.*"

Aanya clutched the letter to her chest, feeling as though Dev's spirit filled the room, his words a bridge connecting past and present. She looked up at Inspector Deshmukh, who wore an expression of solemn understanding.

Inspector Deshmukh's face took on a distant look, his gaze shifting as if peering back through the years, summoning memories buried beneath the weight of time. "There's more to this than I'd realised," he murmured, almost to himself. His voice softened as he continued, "You know, Aanya, your grandmother's story was part of a mystery that haunted this village for decades."

Aanya looked at him, sensing the gravity in his tone. "What do you mean?"

Deshmukh sighed, crossing his arms as he leaned against the damp wall. "There were rumours back then, whispers that reached even our station in Nandipur. Neeraj and Dhaniram were men with connections, and Dev... was caught in the middle of it all. We'd heard hints, talk of Dev's meetings with your grandmother, of them spending time together under the banyan tree. The village elders frowned upon it, and for reasons I didn't fully understand back then, Neeraj and Dhaniram had Dev watched. They hired rough men, village goons, who reported back on Dev's every move."

Deshmukh's eyes clouded as if reliving a part of his own past. "I remember one night, we brought in a couple of those men on unrelated charges. It was a quiet evening, and as we were booking them, one of them casually mentioned Dev. The man was cocky, not thinking much of the boy whose life he'd been tracking. He said Dev's life was like a 'sparrow in a storm'—watched and controlled, with nowhere to go. He talked about a book where they recorded his movements, his meetings with Savitri, even details about his visits to the banyan tree."

Aanya's heart pounded as she listened, her skin prickling with dread. "A book?" she asked, her voice barely a whisper.

Inspector Deshmukh nodded, his brow furrowing. "Yes, they had a small notebook where they kept notes on him. It wasn't just gossip; it was cold, calculated documentation. Every time he left his house, every step he took in the village was recorded. I managed to get my hands on that book after pressing those men for details. It was chilling, to say the least. Pages filled with observations, dates, and times. The goons had no loyalty to anyone, so they talked freely once they were in custody. They told me that Neeraj and Dhaniram believed keeping tabs on Dev would somehow preserve the family's honour, but it felt like more than that. It was as if they feared him, as though he had some power that threatened their control."

Aanya felt a chill run through her. "But if you had the book, why didn't it ever reach my grandmother or my family?"

Deshmukh's expression darkened, his lips pressing into a thin line. "That's the strange part, Aanya. One day, the book vanished from our evidence room. It was there one moment, gone the next. I searched high and low and questioned everyone at the station. No one had any answers, and I always suspected someone with power had arranged for it to disappear. To this day, I don't know who orchestrated it, but I suspect that it was someone close to Neeraj and Dhaniram. Someone who wanted to erase Dev's memory, as though he'd never existed."

Aanya's pulse quickened, the weight of the revelation settling over her like a shroud. "So, they didn't just want him out of the village – they wanted his story erased, his existence wiped clean."

Inspector Deshmukh nodded, his gaze turning sorrowful. "They wanted him gone in every possible way. They couldn't control the love between Dev and Savitri, so they tried to control the narrative. By making him disappear, by silencing him in both life and memory, they thought they could restore what they believed was their honour. But Dev's story was persistent; it lingered like a ghost in the village, and now it has found its way back to the surface."

Inspector Deshmukh was still, his eyes lost in memories, when Rohan reached into his backpack, pulling out a small, weathered notebook. Its cover was scuffed and faded, the pages brittle and yellowed with age. He held it out to the inspector, a quiet intensity in his gaze.

"Is this the book?" Rohan asked, his voice barely a whisper as if he understood the weight of the moment.

Deshmukh's eyes widened as he looked down at the notebook. He reached for it slowly as though afraid it might vanish if he moved too quickly. His fingers brushed the cover reverently, and he opened it, flipping through the pages with a sharp, practised eye. The notes were handwritten, short lines detailing dates, times, and the mundane movements of a life observed from the shadows. Every entry was meticulous, capturing Dev's comings and goings with a chilling detachment.

"Yes," the inspector murmured, a mixture of disbelief and sorrow etched on his face. "This is it. This is the notebook they used to keep tabs on Dev." He shook his head slowly, the anger and sadness of years past surfacing. "I thought this was gone forever. It vanished from the station decades ago, and I always suspected it was taken to erase any trace of Dev's life here. Whoever took it did so to protect a lie, to rewrite history as they wanted it remembered."

Aanya's heart pounded as she watched Inspector Deshmukh examine the notebook, his fingers tracing the delicate, faded ink. It was eerie to see Dev's life laid out in such cold, impersonal detail, the way he was watched, tracked, and his movements reduced to mere lines on a page. The notebook wasn't just evidence of surveillance; it was proof of the relentless pressure Dev had endured, the invisible chains that had bound him to a fate controlled by those who refused to let him be free.

Deshmukh looked up at Rohan and Aanya, a profound sadness in his gaze. "This notebook is more than just an account of his daily movements; it's a record of the way they tried to erase him. Neeraj and Dhaniram couldn't tolerate a love that defied their plans, so they monitored Dev and turned his life into something they could control, something they thought they could suppress."

Aanya's voice trembled as she spoke. "But in trying to erase him, they ended up preserving his story. Every note, every date, it's a testament to how much he meant, to how deeply he threatened the order they were trying to impose."

Deshmukh nodded, closing the notebook with a heavy sigh. "What they didn't understand is that love, especially a love as deep and pure as Dev's, leaves traces that can't be so easily erased. The more they tried to control him, the more his memory persisted, clinging to this village like a ghost. And now, thanks to you, Aanya, Dev's story has found its way back to the light."

He handed the notebook back to Rohan, who tucked it carefully into his backpack. "Keep this safe," Deshmukh said. "It's not just evidence of what they did to Dev; it's a piece of his life, a life they couldn't silence. You've given him a voice again."

Aanya felt a deep sense of purpose settles over her. This notebook, this painful relic of surveillance and control, was now a part of the legacy she would carry forward. Dev's story had been buried, but it would no longer be hidden. With the notebook in hand, she and Rohan had the last piece of the puzzle, a tangible reminder of a love that had been suppressed but had never truly died.

Aanya glanced down at the letter in her hand, Dev's words trembling in her fingers. "Thank you, Inspector," she whispered, her voice thick with emotion. "For remembering, for helping bring this story back to life."

The inspector gave her a solemn nod, his gaze thoughtful as he considered the letter. "Your grandmother's story was never just a tale of love and loss, Aanya. It's a testament to resilience, to love's endurance even in the face of silence. What Neeraj and Dhaniram tried to erase has now been brought into the light."

Aanya's tears spilt over, a bittersweet smile breaking through her sorrow. As they left the haveli, the notebook tucked safely in Rohan's backpack, Aanya carried with her not just the story of Dev and Savitri but a quiet understanding of the love and resilience that had shaped her family's path.

Outside the haveli, Aanya looked up at the fading sky, her heart swelling with a mixture of grief, gratitude, and newfound purpose. She had uncovered a truth that was far more than a hidden love story; she had discovered her grandmother's resilience and, along the way, had uncovered her own strength and capacity to love fiercely.

Rohan turned to her, his expression warm and proud. "You did it, Aanya. You brought them back to life, in a way. Their love isn't a secret anymore. It's part of you, part of your family now."

Aanya looked at him, her voice trembling as she spoke. "Thank you, Rohan. For being here, for helping me find this, for... everything." Her hand tightened around his, a silent promise of all the unspoken feelings between them.

He squeezed her hand, his eyes unwavering. "I wouldn't have been anywhere else. And Aanya... you've honoured their love. Now it's time to honour your own heart, too."

As she held his gaze, Aanya felt the weight of her grandmother's past lifting. She wasn't bound by the silence and secrets that had once held Savitri back. She could love freely, without fear, and move forward, carrying the legacy of the love her grandmother had denied.

For a long moment, they stood hand in hand, gazing at the haveli as if bidding it farewell. Aanya knew her journey wasn't over; it had simply taken on a new shape.

She would carry Dev and Savitri's love with her, but she would also forge her own path, one filled with courage, resilience, and the freedom to live without secrets.

As the first stars appeared in the twilight sky, Aanya took a deep breath. She felt the notebook tucked securely in her bag, the story she had pieced together written within its pages, ready to be told. It was time to go back to Mumbai to face her family and share the legacy she had unearthed. She would show them what she had written, show them the love that had been buried for generations. Her grandmother's story had found its voice, and now, so had hers.

The Breaking Point

B ack in her parents' house, the atmosphere was charged, tense in a way Aanya hadn't felt since she was a teenager. The familiar sights and smells of her childhood home—the wooden shelves filled with family photos, the faint aroma of her mother's incense—felt foreign, almost stifling under the weight of what she had brought with her from Nandipur.

She sat across from her parents in the living room, the diary and letters resting on the table between them, physical reminders of a story that had been hidden for so long. Her father sat rigidly, his knuckles white as he clutched the arm of his chair. Her mother, quiet and pale, glanced at the letters, her lips pressed tightly together.

The air was thick with tension as Aanya's father rose from his chair, his face flushed with anger and something deeper, an old wound resurfacing, one that had lain dormant for years. He paced across the living room, his footsteps heavy against the tiled floor, his eyes fixed on Aanya with a mix of disbelief and frustration.

"Are you telling me," he began, his voice laced with controlled anger, "that your grandmother had some hidden love all these years? That she carried on with this man, Dev, while living with our family, raising us? And you think it's your place to come here and... and romanticise that?"

Aanya felt her own temper flare, the familiar push and pull of her father's judgements pressing down on her. She had expected her family to be surprised, maybe even hurt, but this... this felt like a betrayal of her grandmother's memory. She stood up, meeting her father's gaze head-on, her voice sharp.

"Dad, you don't understand. Dadi didn't 'carry on' with anyone. She loved Dev before you, before any of us. She was forced to make choices none of us can truly understand. This isn't about judging her; it's about recognising the strength it took for her to live with that pain in silence."

He scoffed, shaking his head. "Strength? Is that what you call it? Hiding some... some secret love while pretending to be a devoted mother and wife? Aanya, you're putting her on a pedestal she doesn't deserve. We're her family; why didn't she trust us enough to share this?"

Aanya's voice rose, her frustration bubbling over. "Because she knew you wouldn't understand! She knew that people like you would judge her and would turn her love into something shameful instead of something beautiful. She sacrificed so much for us, and you can't see past your own pride!"

Her father's eyes narrowed, his jaw tightening. "Don't talk to me about sacrifice, Aanya. I spent years taking care of her, giving up things in my own life to make sure she was comfortable, and honouring her. And now, you want me to believe she was hiding some forbidden love all along? You think that's easy for me to accept?"

Aanya clenched her fists, her voice trembling with anger. "No, I don't think it's easy, but it's the truth! She loved him, and just because it doesn't fit into your idea of family loyalty doesn't mean it's wrong. You're so quick to judge her, to judge me for bringing this to light, but you haven't even tried to understand what she went through!"

Her father's face darkened; his voice was cold. "What did she go through? And what about what I went through, Aanya? Growing up with a mother who was always distant, always somewhere else in her mind. We never had her fully, did we? And now you're trying to tell me that's because she was thinking about some other man?"

The words stung, and Aanya felt a rush of anger and hurt that left her struggling to find the right response.

She opened her mouth to speak, but before she could, her mother, Meera, stepped between them, her voice calm yet commanding.

"Enough. Both of you," Meera said, her eyes moving between her husband and daughter, her tone leaving no room for argument. "We are not going to stand here and tear apart a woman who gave her life to this family. You're both hurting, and you're both right in your own ways. But this is not how we honour her memory."

Aanya took a deep breath, her anger simmering down as she looked at her mother. She could see the pain in Meera's eyes, the sadness that lingered beneath her calm demeanour. Her mother had always been the mediator, the one who kept the family together, and now, she was doing the same with her own husband and daughter.

Meera turned to her husband, her voice softer but firm. "She was your mother. And yes, it hurts to know there was a part of her life that we didn't understand. But that doesn't change the fact that she loved you, that she was there for you when you needed her. Don't let this discovery turn you against the memory of the woman who raised you."

Her husband looked away, his face shadowed with unresolved grief and frustration. Meera turned back to Aanya, placing a hand on her shoulder.

"And Aanya, you're right to honour her love, to seek the truth. But you need to understand that this is painful for all of us, not just you. You're asking us to reframe our entire understanding of her, to see her as a woman who lived with this deep, unspoken love. That's not easy."

Aanya looked down, her anger slowly dissolving into a mixture of shame and sorrow. "I… I just wanted you to see her for who she really was, to understand that she was more than just our Dadi. She was a woman who had her own dreams, her own sacrifices."

Meera took a deep breath, her eyes softening as she looked between her husband and her daughter. "Maybe it's time we stop expecting her to fit into the roles we've assigned her. Maybe it's time we let her be the woman she was, fully and honestly."

Aanya's father let out a long sigh, his gaze softening as he met his wife's eyes. "I… I don't know how to make peace with this, Meera. She was my mother. I loved her; I respected her. But this… this makes it feel like I never really knew her."

Meera placed a comforting hand on his arm; her voice filled with understanding. "Maybe none of us truly knew her. But that doesn't change the love she had for us, the life she shared with us. She was human, with complexities we might never fully understand. But that doesn't make her love for us any less real."

Aanya's father looked down, his voice softened with a hint of remorse. "You're right. She gave us everything she could. Maybe it's time I try to see her as more than just the mother I wanted her to be."

Aanya felt a tear slip down her cheek, relief and sorrow mingling as she looked at her parents. "That's all I wanted, Dad. For us to see her fully, to honour everything she was."

Her father gave her a small nod, his face lined with a mix of regret and acceptance. "I'm... sorry, Aanya. I shouldn't have reacted that way. It's just... hard. But I see now why you did this, why you needed us to know."

They stood in silence, a sense of resolution settling over them, as they began to see Savitri not through the lens of her sacrifices but as a woman of quiet resilience who had shaped their lives with unwavering love. Her strength was no longer a mystery but a legacy, one that would guide them in ways they were only starting to grasp.

Aanya's father finally exhaled, his shoulders softening as he reached out and gently took the diary from Aanya's hands. He studied its worn leather cover, his thumb tracing the edges where time had faded the material. "This little book," he murmured, his voice thick with emotion, "held so much of her. And we never knew."

Aanya stepped closer, feeling a quiet pride that her father had finally accepted this part of Savitri's story.

"Dadi wanted us to find this when the time was right. Maybe she knew we'd understand better once we were ready to see her as more than just our Dadi."

Her father nodded, looking at Aanya with a softened gaze. "You were the one she chose to reveal her truth, Aanya. It must have been a heavy responsibility, but... I see now why she entrusted it to you."

Aanya swallowed, her voice tender with emotion. "I think she saw a bit of herself in me. The part of her that wanted to live fully, to love without boundaries, even if she couldn't. I don't want her sacrifices to go unrecognised. I don't want her story to be just whispers or memories in an old house."

Her mother, Meera, reached out, wrapping an arm around Aanya. "And it won't be, beta. You've brought her story to life. You've made her memory whole again. Her love, her pain, her strength – it's all part of who we are now. And we're stronger for it."

The quiet room was filled with a warmth that seemed to pulse with Savitri's presence as if she were standing among them, proud and grateful. Her secrets, once buried, now breathed freely, binding her family together with a love that transcended time and silence.

As they sat together, sharing memories of Savitri—her laughter, her quiet wisdom, the way she would braid Aanya's hair or hum old songs while cooking—Aanya felt a weight lift from her heart. This was the closure she had been seeking, not only for herself but for her grandmother, for the life she had lived in quiet dignity and hidden sorrow.

Her father cleared his throat, his tone thoughtful as he addressed Aanya. "You know... this guy, Rohan. You've mentioned him a few times. He sounds like a good person, someone who's been by your side through all this."

Aanya blushed, caught off guard by the sudden change in conversation. "Yes, he... he's been there every step of the way. I think... I think Dadi's story has shown me that love can be complicated, that it can be quiet and steadfast. And Rohan, he... he makes me feel like I don't have to hide any part of myself."

Her mother smiled knowingly, squeezing her hand. "Then don't hide, Aanya. Don't let love slip by because of fear or hesitation. Dadi had to live with silence, with hidden love. But you—" her voice softened, filled with gentle encouragement, "you can embrace it fully."

Aanya's father nodded, a small, approving smile on his face. "We may not have all the answers, but I know this: your grandmother wouldn't want you to carry her burdens. She'd want you to live boldly, to love without fear."

Aanya's eyes filled with gratitude as she looked at her family, the love and understanding that bound them now stronger than ever. She felt a sense of freedom, of having come full circle, her heart open to possibilities she had once been afraid to consider.

The night continued in warmth and shared stories, their laughter echoing through the room as they remembered Savitri not just as the quiet matriarch but as a woman who had poured her heart into her family, giving everything to ensure their happiness and strength. Aanya knew that wherever her grandmother was, she would be smiling, content in the knowledge that her story was no longer a secret but a cherished part of the family's legacy.

As she sat beside her family, Aanya's thoughts drifted to Rohan. Her journey had brought her to a place of understanding, a place where she could finally love with an open heart, free from fear or hesitation. She had found not only her grandmother's story but her own as well, one that was filled with courage, resilience, and the kind of love that transcends silence.

And as the night faded into dawn, Aanya knew that she was ready to embrace whatever lay ahead, honouring her grandmother's memory by living fully, openly, with a heart unburdened and free.

A New Beginning

Aanya stood in the bustling café in Mumbai, scanning the room until her eyes found Rohan seated at a corner table by the window. The familiar sight of him—a notebook open beside his coffee, his gaze focused as he jotted down notes—filled her with a warmth that she could hardly contain. As if sensing her presence, Rohan looked up and broke into a smile, a look of genuine happiness spreading across his face. She felt her heart race, the weight of all they'd been through together resting between them like a silent promise.

"Hey," she greeted, sliding into the chair across from him. The noise of the café faded into the background, and for a moment, it felt like it was just the two of them in the world.

"Aanya," Rohan said, his voice filled with a mixture of joy and relief. "It's good to see you here, back in the city. How are you... really?"

She smiled a little nervously, realising how much she had missed him in these past few days since her return. "I'm... different," she admitted, the understatement making them both chuckle. "I think we all are. It's been a strange time for my family, but I think we're finally starting to heal. The truth about Dadi, her story–it's brought us closer, made us understand her and each other in ways I didn't think were possible."

Rohan's eyes softened as he reached across the table, his hand brushing hers in a gentle, comforting gesture. "I'm glad. Your Dadi... she's become so real to me, too. And I think wherever she is, she's proud of you for doing what you did."

Aanya looked down at their entwined hands, her heart filling with gratitude and something deeper, something she had been afraid to acknowledge until now. "It hasn't been easy. Dad struggled to accept it, but Mom... she's been incredible. She helped us all see Dadi for who she truly was, as more than just a mother or a grandmother, but as a woman who had her own dreams, her own struggles."

She paused, gathering her thoughts, feeling a mix of courage and vulnerability welling up inside her. "I don't think I could have done this without you, Rohan. You were there every step of the way. You saw me through every moment of doubt, of anger, of heartbreak. You were my rock."

Rohan's expression softened, his thumb tracing gentle circles on the back of her hand. "I wouldn't have been anywhere else, Aanya. Seeing you uncover your grandmother's story, watching you grow... it was one of the most beautiful things I've ever witnessed."

Aanya swallowed, her heart pounding as she met his gaze. She felt a vulnerability she hadn't felt in years, a feeling that was both terrifying and exhilarating. Taking a steadying breath, she finally let the words slip past her lips.

"Rohan, I think I've been falling for you since the moment we started this journey together. I was afraid to admit it, afraid that maybe... maybe I was just clinging to you because of everything we'd been through. But I know now that it's more than that. I love you."

Rohan's face lit up, his eyes filled with a warmth that made her heart swell. He gently squeezed her hand, his voice steady but filled with emotion. "Aanya, I love you too. I think I've known it for a while now, but I didn't want to say anything, not until I was sure you were ready to hear it. You've been through so much, and I didn't want to add any pressure."

Aanya's cheeks flushed, a mixture of relief and joy washing over her. "This journey, finding Dadi's story... it taught me that life is too short to hold back. She spent her whole life with a love that was hidden, a love that was beautiful but silent. I don't want that for us, Rohan. I want to be brave enough to love fully, openly."

Rohan smiled, his gaze filled with admiration. "I want that too, Aanya. And I promise, whatever comes our way, I'll be right here by your side."

They sat in comfortable silence, the weight of their shared journey resting between them, transformed now into a bond that was undeniable, a love that felt strong enough to weather any storm. They had seen each other at their most vulnerable, had walked through grief and discovery together, and had emerged on the other side, stronger, closer, ready to build something real.

Rohan reached into his bag, pulling out a small journal with a soft leather cover. "I started this while we were in Nandipur. I thought... maybe someday, we'd want to look back and remember everything we went through. The moments we shared, the things we discovered... even the hard parts."

Aanya took the journal, her fingers brushing over its cover, and opened it, seeing Rohan's neat handwriting filling the pages. Each entry held memories of the journey they'd taken, reflections, sketches, and observations. As she turned the pages, she felt herself transported back through each moment they had shared, each fragment of their journey in Nandipur. It was a testament to the love that had grown quietly between them, a love rooted in shared discoveries, in comforting silences, in the unspoken understanding that had blossomed through each challenge they faced together.

The first entry made her smile: a sketch of the train they had taken to Nandipur. Rohan had drawn the two of them seated side by side, Aanya gazing out of the window as he jotted observations in his notebook. She remembered the nervous excitement she had felt on that journey, the sense of stepping into the unknown. And even then, without fully realising it, she had felt safe with him, his quiet presence reassuring her that she wouldn't be facing this alone.

Her eyes lingered on his words beside the sketch.

"*A quiet peace settles over the journey, with her by my side, leaning against the window as the countryside blurs past. I can see the anticipation in her eyes, the courage she doesn't yet know she has. I wonder if she realises how strong she is.*"

Aanya felt her throat tighten, moved by how deeply he had seen her, even in those early days. She turned to the next page, where he had written about the banyan tree. Her fingers traced his careful lines.

"*The banyan tree. She stood there, lost in thought, her fingers brushing the bark as if trying to reach across time. I don't know what she was feeling, but I could feel her heartache, her need for answers. There's a beauty in her vulnerability, in the way she carries this legacy with so much care. I wanted to reach out, to hold her hand, to let her know she wasn't alone."*

Reading those words, Aanya felt as if she were standing under the banyan tree once again, the weight of her grandmother's memories pressing against her. She had felt alone, burdened by the secrets she had been uncovering, but Rohan had been there, steady and unwavering, offering his quiet support. She hadn't needed to ask him to stay; he had simply been there as if he had always belonged by her side.

Page after page, Rohan's words unfolded their journey, capturing both the smallest moments and the profound realisations they had shared. A sketch of her silhouette against the faded blue walls of her grandmother's house, where he had written:

"She stood in the doorway, her gaze distant but determined, as if she could see the past unfolding before her. I've never seen anyone carry so much weight with so much grace. Being here, watching her, I feel something I can't yet put into words. I just know I'd follow her anywhere."

Aanya felt her heart swell, warmth spreading through her as she realised just how deeply he had cared for her, even from the beginning. His words captured her journey, yes, but they also reflected his own journey, the quiet strength he had found in supporting her, in standing by her through each moment of doubt, fear, and hope.

Finally, she reached the last entry, a simple sketch of her asleep against his shoulder during one of their last train rides back to Mumbai. The lines were soft, capturing her peaceful expression, the small crease of worry that lingered even in her sleep. Beside it, he had written:

"She's done so much, uncovered so many truths. I see the relief in her now, the peace settling over her. I know she'll keep going, but I also know she's ready to rest, to let herself breathe. I hope she knows that whatever path she chooses next, I'll be there by her side."

Tears welled up in her eyes, her fingers lingering over the words, tracing them as if they held some deeper magic. She looked up at him, her voice thick with emotion.

"Rohan... I didn't know you felt all this. I didn't realise... you saw me this way."

He smiled softly, his gaze steady, filled with warmth and quiet intensity. "Aanya, you are everything I saw and more. I wrote these words not just to remember our journey but because... I didn't know how else to tell you how much I care. How much you mean to me."

Aanya felt her breath catch as she looked into his eyes, feeling the strength of his love wrap around her, a love that was patient, gentle, and unyielding. She closed the journal, holding it close to her chest as if it were a part of him, a part of them. "Rohan, I... I love you. I've tried to be careful, to protect myself, but you've shown me that love doesn't have to be hidden. That it can be quiet and still be everything."

Rohan reached across the table, taking her hands in his, his gaze unwavering. "Aanya, I love you too. I've loved you in every moment, in every step we took together. And I want us to keep walking, to keep building something beautiful together."

They sat in silence for a moment, the weight of their confessions settling between them, a promise unspoken but deeply felt. Aanya felt a joy she hadn't known was possible, a lightness that came from knowing she was finally allowing herself to be fully seen, fully loved. She no longer carried her grandmother's story as a burden but as a bridge, a connection to a love that had shaped her own.

"What do we do now?" she asked, a soft laugh escaping her, a mixture of nervousness and excitement.

Rohan's smile grew, his eyes crinkling with warmth. "We keep writing, Aanya. We keep telling our story, just as we started. And whatever comes next, we face it together."

They left the café hand in hand, stepping out into the bustling streets of Mumbai. The city pulsed around them, alive with noise and colour, but Aanya felt only the steady beat of her own heart, finally free, finally open.

As they walked, Aanya knew that this was just the beginning. The journey they had shared had brought them here, but now, they were writing their own chapter – a chapter filled with the courage to love deeply, the strength to honour the past, and the promise of a future they would build together.

Epilogue: Whispers in Ink

Anya sat at her desk, the soft morning light spilling across her open journal. The quiet of the early hour wrapped around her like a gentle reminder of the journey she had taken and the stories that had come to define her. She had filled pages with memories of a woman she'd known as her grandmother, a woman whose love story had been a secret for so long that it almost felt like a myth. But now, the tale was alive again, woven into words that gave it breath, echoing in her heart and in the lives of those she loved.

She smiled to herself, a warmth settling over her as she wrote.

"Dadi's love was a quiet strength, an unspoken truth carried through years of separation and silence. She loved a man she could never truly have, yet she never let that loss harden her. Instead, she built a life around her family, pouring love into her children and her home while keeping

that part of her heart hidden and sacred. Her story taught me that love is not bound by words or time; it exists, whether we give it voice or not. "

Aanya paused, glancing at the ring on her finger, a reminder of her own love story with Rohan. He had given her the courage to live freely, to embrace love without fear or hesitation. Their love had been shaped by quiet moments, by whispered conversations under starry skies, by shared secrets that had bound them together. Rohan had shown her that love didn't have to remain hidden, it could be a part of every day, every laugh, every promise made and kept.

She continued writing, her pen flowing easily across the page.

"I've learned that love, in all its forms, shapes us. Sometimes, it's a gentle whisper, sometimes a radiant light. But whether quiet or bold, love brings us closer to who we are meant to be, giving us the strength to live truthfully and openly. Dadi's strength was in her silence, in the resilience it took to carry a love that would never be fulfilled. My strength, I've realised, is in my voice, in my choice to live and love fully. "

Her thoughts drifted to Dev, to the letters he had left behind, the final words he had written to Savitri. His love had survived exile, had lingered in memories he had held close to his heart. Dev's fate, however, remained a mystery.

Had he lived out his days thinking of her, holding her in his heart just as she had carried him in hers? Or had he found peace in another life, in another place?

Aanya smiled softly, imagining him somewhere, a gentle shadow in the background of her grandmother's life. She wondered if he had ever returned to Nandipur if he had stood under the banyan tree again, the same tree where they had once dreamed of a future that was never meant to be. Did he ever look back? She wondered and remembered.

She let her pen move once more, capturing the lessons she had learned from Dadi's story and her own journey.

"To love fully, I have learned, is to live without fear. To let love guide us, whether it speaks in whispers or stands boldly in the light. Dadi's love may have lived in silence, but it led me to my own truth, my own heart. Through her, I found the courage to love openly, to embrace the life that is mine."

She leaned back, feeling a quiet peace settle within her. Her grandmother's story was no longer a secret; it was a legacy, one she would carry forward, a testament to the quiet strength that had shaped her family. And though she might never know what had become of Dev, she knew that his love had left an imprint on her life, guiding her towards a deeper understanding of what it meant to live authentically.

Aanya rose from her desk, joining Rohan in the kitchen where he was pouring their morning coffee. He looked up with a warm smile, handing her a cup, his fingers brushing hers.

"Finished writing for today?" he asked, his voice soft, knowing the weight of what she had put down on the page.

She nodded, smiling back. "Yes. I think I finally understand Dadi's story, her choices, and her strength. And I understand myself better because of her."

Rohan wrapped an arm around her, pulling her close. "She'd be so proud of you, Aanya. You've honoured her memory beautifully, and you've carried her story forward in a way that no one else could."

Aanya leaned into him, feeling the warmth of his embrace. For the first time, she felt truly at peace, her heart free of questions, her soul filled with gratitude. Her grandmother's love story had shaped her own, teaching her to embrace life fully, to live with her heart open, unafraid of the complexities that love often brings.

As they stood together, watching the morning unfold, Aanya knew that her journey wasn't just about uncovering her grandmother's past; it was about finding the courage to live her own life with honesty and grace. She had learned to let love be her guide, to let it shape her in quiet moments and in bright declarations, just as Dadi's love had done for her.

And as she looked up at Rohan, her heart full, she knew their story was just beginning – a story of love that would continue to grow, shaped by the legacy of those who had come before them.

With a smile, she thought of her grandmother's wisdom, of the strength it had taken to love quietly, steadfastly, through years of silence. And as her thoughts drifted to Dev, to the mystery of his life, there was one lingering question:

"Perhaps Dev's story didn't end in Nandipur. Perhaps somewhere, he carried her memory as she carried his, each bound to the other in quiet resilience, leaving whispers in the wind."

As her thoughts wandered back to Rohan, Aanya felt a quiet certainty settle within her. Her story, like her grandmother's, would live on, carried forward with courage, bound by love, and lived with an open heart.

One profound lesson this journey had etched into her heart was this: *Love shapes us—sometimes in silence, sometimes in light—but always guiding us toward our most authentic selves.*

Made in the USA
Las Vegas, NV
11 February 2025

17874643R10125